RISING TIDE

Books by Jean Thesman

Rising Tide
Between
A Sea So Far
In the House of the Queen's Beasts
Calling the Swan
The Other Ones
The Tree of Bells
The Moonstones
The Storyteller's Daughter
The Ornament Tree
Summerspell
Cattail Moon
Nothing Grows Here
Molly Donnelly
When the Road Ends
The Rain Catchers
Appointment with a Stranger
Rachel Chance
The Last April Dancers

RISING TIDE

Jean Thesman

VIKING

VIKING
Published by Penguin Group
Penguin Young Readers Group, 345 Hudson Street, New York, New York 10014, U.S.A.
Penguin Books Ltd, 80 Strand, London WC2R 0RL, England
Penguin Books Australia Ltd, 250 Camberwell Road, Camberwell, Victoria 3124, Australia
Penguin Books Canada Ltd, 10 Alcorn Avenue, Toronto, Ontario, Canada M4V 3B2
Penguin Books (N.Z.) Ltd, 182-190 Wairau Road, Auckland 10, New Zealand

First published in 2003 by Viking, a division of Penguin Young Readers Group

10 9 8 7 6 5 4 3 2 1

LIBRARY OF CONGRESS CATALOGING-IN-PUBLICATION DATA
Thesman, Jean.
Rising tide / Jean Thesman.
p. cm.
Sequel to: A sea so far.
Summary: In 1908, Kate and Ellen set up shop and begin to sell handmade
Irish linens to a select San Francisco clientele.
ISBN 0-670-03656-0 (hardcover)
[1. Entrepreneurship—Fiction. 2. Sex role—Fiction. 3. Boardinghouses—Fiction.
4. San Francisco (Calif.)—History—20th century—Fiction.] I. Title.
PZ7.T3525Ri 2003 [Fic]—dc21 2003001381

Printed in U.S.A.
Set in Caslon
Book design by Nancy Brennan

To Basha Jackson, musician, for her support
and for her contribution to my gardens.

And to Jean Immerwahr, poet, for her timeless advice,
and for an invitation to a perfect luncheon.

RISING TIDE

Chapter 1
KATE
December 1908

"Kate, look at that!"

Katherine Keely looked up from her travel journal when Annie Prescott cried out, to catch a glimpse of a bonfire through the train window. But it was out of sight before she saw it clearly, and the train curved away along the track, moving south through the late evening toward California and home.

The sight of fire often made her uneasy, but Annie interrupted her worry by saying, "I saw dozens of children gathered around. It must be an early Christmas celebration. What fun!"

Kate's rigid spine relaxed. A celebration, not devastation. She had never completely recovered from the great San Francisco fire that had followed the earthquake more than two years before, and sometimes open flames triggered terrible memories. She never spoke of them, however. Few of the victims ever did.

"It's hard to think about Christmas when you're on a train," Kate said.

"We'll be home in time for it," Annie said. She smiled across the compartment at Kate and then went back to her book.

The train swayed just enough to cause Kate's pencil to add unexpected flourishes in her small leather journal, but she was accustomed to this. She and the Prescotts, her friends and traveling companions, had left New York four days earlier, and even though she had known the trip would be miserable in winter, she had not expected spending so many hours waiting for rails to be cleared of snow, or being sidetracked when a wealthy man's private train needed their engines to help it speed through a mountain pass, or encountering the beggars-turned-robbers who piled on the car ahead of hers at a meal stop, assaulting passengers and demanding money and jewelry before the men in the car overpowered them and threw them out. There was a great deal to put in a journal.

Kate, in the process of recording what she knew of the attempted robbery, paused long enough to look out the window again at the deepening twilight, and shook her head slowly. Perhaps the travel difficulties had been for the best after all. She had not had much time to worry about the uncertainty that was waiting for her in San Francisco or to brood about the tragedy she had left behind in Ireland.

The plans for independence that she had made while she was in Dublin might not work out now. She had been hired to care for Jolie Logan—and promised a reward for staying with the young invalid—but Jolie, who had become her close friend, had died in spite of everything. Now Kate was left in the kind of position she had always hated, unable to see a clear path ahead of her. How could she provide a living for her aunt and herself? Travel problems might even be looked at as a relief, since dealing with the delays, the noise, the smells, and the exasperation of being trapped in a car with mostly incompatible strangers offered an odd kind of diversion.

Kate's compartment door opened and Annie's husband, Peter, came in with news. "We'll be stopping in half an hour for dinner. Annie and I know this place very well, Kate. The food is good, and you must eat something this time. You've grown so thin that your aunt will think we broke our promise and didn't take care of you on the way home."

Kate closed the black leather journal, slipped it into her skirt pocket, and stood up stiffly. She had left Dublin for home in November and had spent nearly a week in cramped quarters aboard ship, then two weeks in a New York hotel waiting while Peter recovered from a particularly serious case of influenza, and then this train trip that seemed endless. Who wanted to eat? "I'll enjoy food more when I'm back in San Francisco," she said. She made a small effort to tidy her curly red hair, gave up, and asked Annie for help. "Aunt Grace always tells me that I look like a banshee."

Annie laughed, touched her own curly hair, and then took the brush that Kate handed her. "I hate my hair until I see someone struggling with curl papers or a crimping iron. There, now. You look fine. I'll get out my heavy coat—it's going to be cold at the station—and then perhaps I'll go visit with your new friends until we stop. What nice girls! We should all get together for dinner some time soon."

Kate, settling her small black hat in place, said, "I don't know how you do it. You must know people all over the world."

But Annie only laughed again. "We love to make new friends when we travel. And we'll travel for the rest of our lives, I hope."

Kate, almost eighteen, never wanted to leave California again. She had departed San Francisco in May, originally expecting to be home within six months, and was now barely able to hope that she would celebrate Christmas with her aunt. "You're braver than I," she said.

Annie paused, her coat slung over one arm. "No one is braver than you, Kate."

Kate looked down for a moment, long enough to be sure that her eyes would not fill with tears. "The hardest part is yet to come. I have to talk to Jolie's father about everything, and I dread it so much."

"He's had your cables and the telegrams you sent from New York," Peter protested. "And surely Jolie's aunt must have cabled him, too."

"But he'll want to know why I gave in to her demands and left her aunt's house when she was so ill," Kate said. She pulled her coat on over her jacket and picked up her gloves. "I guess we'd better get ready."

Kate and Annie had shared a compartment since they left New York, changing trains and enduring endless waits on platforms that all looked the same to Kate. Peter had always arranged to have a berth near their door, and during the day he often spent hours with them in the compartment. But Kate, restless and sick of travel, had changed places with him for several hours each morning, and so she had met two young women, Edith Jones and Adele Carson, who were moving from New York to San Francisco.

The passengers were stirring, gathering up heavy wraps. The air smelled of coal smoke coming from the inefficient heating stoves, kerosene lanterns, cigars, and travel-stained clothing. Kate looked forward to taking deep breaths as soon as she left the car. Cold, deep breaths. Perhaps she was hungry after all.

Edith and Adele smiled when they saw her. "Are you

feeling better now, Kate?" asked Edith, the bride-to-be who had been willing to cross a continent to marry an old friend who was doing well in the business of rebuilding San Francisco.

Kate assured Edith that she had had a chance to rest, although that had not been strictly the case. Adele got up and pulled her heavy cape off the back of her red velvet seat, settling it around her shoulders. She was younger than Edith, closer to Kate's age, and she was planning to live with her grandparents in San Francisco. "They're awfully stuffy, but anything is better than working in a New York shirtwaist factory," she had told Kate.

The train stopped at a small station platform, where the frozen slush was stained black from coal dust, and two dozen beggars wrapped in blankets and rags watched sullenly. There was a delay before the passengers were let off, and the porter told them that someone had been injured in the robbery and now was being taken off the train for belated medical treatment. At last they were set free. The passengers hurried to find dinner, most turning their faces away from the outstretched dirty hands. The beggars at the first stations on the journey west had evoked pity. By now the travelers were leery of them, especially after the attack on the people in the other car.

Peter steered his wife, Kate, and her new friends toward a restaurant he knew very well, and they settled themselves at a long table where Peter ordered for them all.

The meal was served promptly, which was a good thing because they had only forty-five minutes to eat and return to the train. Kate was hungry after all, and she ate fried pork chops and stewed tomatoes with more enthusiasm than she could have imagined earlier.

"Two days to Christmas," Adele said, as she folded her napkin and put it beside her empty plate. "I promised my grandparents that I'd be there in time to celebrate with them. But I heard the conductor say that there had been snow slides ahead of us."

Peter shook his head. "Don't say something like that aloud. I'm determined that we'll be home tomorrow, right on schedule."

"That still leaves enough time for the train to be derailed," Adele said, and everyone laughed, although Kate had to force herself to join in. She knew she might enjoy talking about this trip one day, but not yet. Not yet.

They stumbled back to the train platform over frozen ruts of mud and snow. The beggars were still on the platform, deliberately jostling passengers as they attempted to board. A woman wrapped in a filthy shawl grabbed at Kate's sleeve, but Peter intervened, ordering the woman to let go. Kate rushed up the steps and inside the car.

"Here, Kate!" Peter called out, close behind her. "Isn't this yours?" He held out the small leather travel journal.

"Did that woman have it?" Kate asked, surprised. She had made the skirt she was wearing, and the pockets were deep and concealed in the side seams to protect her from pickpockets.

"No, it was lying on the snow," Peter said. "Unless she had it and then dropped it."

The passengers crowded before and behind Kate, and she was moved along through the car, unable to examine the journal until she reached her compartment. And then she saw, astonished, that it was not hers.

Peter shut the compartment door behind Kate and Annie and threw off his coat. "I'll sit with you ladies for a while," he said. "What's wrong, Kate?"

Kate held up the opened journal. "This isn't mine," she said. She showed it to Peter and Annie. "See? It's just like it, though."

"Is there a name inside?" Annie asked, looking over Kate's shoulder.

Kate examined the first pages. "No, no name. Not even initials." She handed the journal back to Peter and said, "You'd better ask the people in the car. I know I'd hate to lose my journal. Somebody's probably missing it already."

Peter left again, and while he was gone, the porter came to make up the two beds in the compartment. Peter returned, still holding the small black book. "No one claimed it," he said. "It's possible that it belongs to someone in another car, but the porters are making up the berths now, so I'll find the owner tomorrow. Can I do anything for either of you?"

"We're fine," Annie told him. "One more night in the train, and after that we'll have beds that don't sway. But I'm not sure I'll be able to sleep then."

Kate, thinking of the small room she would share with her aunt in the Flannery boardinghouse, smiled to herself. She would be grateful for it, after being confined in even smaller places for so long. Best of all was the chance that she and her aunt might find an apartment she could afford in bustling, extravagant San Francisco and have their own home. It would be possible—if Jolie Logan's father still intended to give her the money he had promised when she had agreed to go to Ireland with his daughter.

Kate had never told anyone about the promise, thank goodness, because now she was not sure she had earned it. Dr. Logan's intention was that Jolie would be launched as a full-time traveler, like the Prescotts. But he had not faced the truth about her health.

Kate, trying to shake creases out of her hopelessly wrinkled travel suit, sighed. Whether she got the money or not, she would have to find a way to earn enough to support her aunt and herself. Aunt Grace had encouraged her and Ellen Flannery to open a small shop and be independent—and Kate and Ellen were saving money toward that goal—but San Francisco was expensive, and never more so than now, while it was rebuilding. The small combined savings of the girls might not be enough to rent a shop, even for a short while. Kate desperately needed Dr. Logan's help.

But his chronically ill daughter had died within hours of Kate's leaving her, and who knew whether or not he would hold her responsible?

"What was the big sigh for?" Annie asked as she brushed her hair.

Kate shivered and crawled into her narrow bed. "I'm just tired, I guess," she said. "And homesick. I'm close enough to San Francisco now to admit it."

They had breakfast the next morning in a hotel dining room near the station, eating quickly because the service had been slow and reluctant. Peter had asked as many passengers as he could find about the journal, but no one claimed it.

"It's yours now, Kate," he said, pushing it across the table to her.

"I don't feel right about taking it," she said slowly. "You're the one who found it."

"I read a few pages last night," Peter confessed. "You're the right one to take charge of it. Only you, Kate."

"Why?" Kate asked, surprised. She opened the journal and looked down at the unfamiliar, angular handwriting.

"Because the writer is also a reluctant traveler, Kate," Peter said. "You'll find a soul mate on the pages."

Kate made a small face. "Soul mate," she said. "How do you know the writer is a man?"

"Women don't usually complain about the quality of their cigars," Peter said, and he and Annie laughed.

Back on the train, she traded seats with Peter and opened the stranger's journal. She felt as if she was prying—and of course she was—so she read the first entry with a flushed face.

Boston. I visited my brother's grave on the day I arrived. The leaves on the nearby trees were burning red and yellow against a lonely gray sky, and after a while a bitter wind tore some of them loose. Boston is so far away from home, and the ocean is all wrong, supporting sunrise instead of sunset. Jeffrey commented on that in a letter once, saying that it depressed him. I wondered if he thought of it at the end.

His lawyer was with me, and we went to the stonecutter's to arrange for a headstone, which will not be set in place until after I have left. I feel guilty for not staying, but October is nearly over, and I want to be home before travel becomes even more difficult.

My brother's affairs took a week to conclude, and on the last day the lawyer offered me a cigar, which I accepted, although I suspected that it would be vile. It was. But then, I am not a smoker. Jeffrey was. My brother was many things that I am not.

But his life has been finished, as if he were a book

someone read and put aside. Now I am all that is left of the family. I had sworn to myself that I would not seek out Isabel, but I went to her uncle's house against my better judgment, where I learned that she had left immediately after Jeffrey died and returned to her parents.

I packed up those things of Jeffrey's that I wanted to keep and arranged to have them shipped home. He had a small blank leather journal that I decided to use myself on the journey back. Who knows—perhaps I shall have a profound thought or two. Or perhaps, with luck, the trip will be too boring to record.

I am far from home and homesick.

Kate shut the journal abruptly and tucked it into her pocket, next to her own journal. How sad, she thought. Another person counting the days.

Kate got off the train in Oakland late on the day before Christmas. Her aunt was waiting for her, crying and reaching out for a hug. The entire Flannery family was there, too, with Ellen laughing as she hugged Kate, and Hugh, red-faced and wearing a stiff new suit, clasping her hand so hard that she winced. Mrs. Flannery and young Joe pushed close to Kate to welcome her home, and Mrs. Flannery added, "I won't believe you're here until we're on the ferry."

"I won't believe it until I unpack," Kate said.

She wondered where the journal writer was that night,

as she crossed San Francisco Bay toward the city where she had been born. Was he home at last, or had he another journey waiting for him before he saw familiar faces again? She would read his journal—probably—but not for a while. She did not even want to look through her own. Half smiling, she wondered if she had finally reached a place in her life when she would be glad to be bored.

In the last moments on the ferry, she waved at Adele and Edith, caught in the crowd and too far away to introduce to her friends, and then her eyes turned to the city lights. Home.

She was so tired that she was barely aware of the trip in the automobile Hugh had borrowed from friends for the occasion. Ellen had chattered constantly the whole way out Market Street from the ferry dock, in spite of her mother's admonitions to hush, and Aunt Grace never let loose of Kate's hand. Young Joe Flannery, sitting in front between his mother and Hugh, gawked over the back of the seat and grinned, showing big teeth, every time Kate spoke.

Here they were. The big, shabby boardinghouse had never seemed more inviting. Hugh helped Kate from the automobile and she looked up—to see a new face watching from the window over the porch.

"Is that a new boarder?" Kate said as she started up the porch steps beside Mrs. Flannery and her aunt, while the Flannery children carried her suitcases.

"Oh, that's just Thalia Rutledge," Aunt Grace said. "I

wrote you about the family. Here, dear, hurry inside where it's warm."

"What kind of name is Thalia?" Mrs. Flannery muttered. "It's foolish. And so are her parents. What was wrong with just plain old 'Polly'?"

"Oh, Ma, what do you care?" Ellen protested irritably. "She can't help what her parents call her. They're actors! Let the kid alone."

Home, Kate thought. And nothing had changed. She smiled.

But Thalia Rutledge, watching from a darkened landing on the stairs, was not smiling.

Chapter 2
ELLEN

Long afterward, that Christmas of 1908 would remain a jumble of mixed memories for Ellen, some happy and some painful. Exhausted, her friend Kate had returned to San Francisco late Christmas Eve and was bundled to bed, leaving Ellen, Ma, Kate's aunt, a boarder named Mrs. Stackhouse, and Mary Clare, the cook, sitting in the kitchen over teacups, speculating—and feeling somewhat let down after all of the excitement.

"Kate looked awful," Mary Clare said as she refilled the cups. "And wasn't she worn down to a nub?" She put down the pot, sighed heavily, and eased herself into a chair. "My mother always said that Dublin can do that to anybody."

The women laughed, but then Ma sobered and said, "It wasn't Dublin. It was Jolie Logan slowly dying the way she did. That would take the spirit out of anybody, even somebody like our Kate."

"Well, Kate should have refused to go to Ireland,"

Ellen said. "Jolie's father knew Jolie was sick. The trip was foolish, right from the start."

"Dr. Logan wanted his girl to go," Ma said, as she shoved a plate of sliced pound cake across the table to Miss Keely. "Take another piece, dearie. No, take that big one." Then she handed the plate to Mrs. Stackhouse and resumed her story. "But Mrs. Conner—she's his housekeeper—she says that Dr. Logan is blaming himself now and hardly ever leaves his house these days."

"Shame on him for feeling sorry for himself. Who is taking care of his patients, then, I'd like to know?" asked Mrs. Stackhouse indignantly. Dr. Logan had been her physician for years.

"Other doctors from the hospital are taking over for him," Ma said.

"Think of him caring so much about his daughter, when You-Know-Who didn't even care enough about theirs to take her along with them to Los Angeles," Miss Keely said, sighing. "I can hear Thalia crying at night sometimes, when I go down the hall."

"How long has it been since the Rutledges left?" Mrs. Stackhouse asked, leaning forward and lowering her voice. "Must be nearly a month."

"And Christmas is almost here, and hardly a blessed word from them selfish people," Mary Clare said. "Not a gift, not a letter, nothing but a postcard with palm trees on it. I've seen her sorting the mail on the hall table, going through it two times to make sure she didn't miss anything. It's enough to make a cow cry."

"Actors," Ma said disgustedly. "What do you expect from people who curl their three-year-old boy's hair with a crimping iron and take him off to that place to put him in one of those Nickelodeon things. 'Baby Cowboys'! That's what Mrs. Rutledge said they were calling it. I'd Baby Cowboy her! And the rent's up at the end of the month, too. Then what?"

"Everything will work out," Ellen said wearily. She felt sorry for Thalia Rutledge, not only because of the twelve-year-old girl's peculiar parents but also because Ma, for some strange reason, was not particularly friendly to the lonely, scrawny child. "The family will come back and move out, and you won't have to think about them any longer."

"They can't move soon enough to suit me," Ma said. "But listen, ladies. Mrs. Conner says Dr. Logan is even thinking of moving over to his place in Marin County and selling the big house. Just think of San Francisco without a Logan in the old Logan house."

That news struck everyone silent.

But why shouldn't the doctor sell the house, Ellen wondered later, as she was getting ready for bed in the room she now shared with her mother, since the boardinghouse was so full. Mrs. Logan had died in the earthquake, and Jolie had died in Ireland. Rattling around in a huge empty house would be awful.

But would it? Even this late at night, she could hear voices and laughter—was that her younger brother, Joe?—through the walls, footsteps on the front and back stairs, running water, and slamming doors. Ma was still downstairs in the kitchen with Mary Clare, and Ellen thought she even heard a kettle hit the floor and an exclamation from the cook. Yes, having a mansion all to herself sounded like paradise. And real servants, not just poor, clumsy Mary Clare bumbling around, spilling things or weeping over burned toast and sad romance serials running in magazines. And not having to endure Mrs. Stackhouse, the boardinghouse sneak, creeping around and eavesdropping on Ellen's telephone conversations.

Ellen hung her clothes in the small closet and pulled hairpins out of her thick, dark hair. Frowning, she sat on the edge of her narrow bed facing the small mirror over the dressing table and brushed her hair a hundred strokes, watching her reflection. She was pretty and she knew it, but what good was that? Money was better. A girl could be as ugly as a dusty old hat and still move in the right circle, if her family was wealthy. Of course, a beautiful girl might marry a rich man, but marriage was the last thing Ellen wanted. Someone bossing her around—and all those babies! That was not for her, at least not before she was thirty. And wouldn't Ma be shocked if she said it aloud. But life had enough worries in it without taking on the additional ones that go with marriage. Just worrying about money alone could make a girl old before it was time.

Sooner or later Kate would want to talk about the plans they had made to rent a shop and sell the linens made in the factory owned by Jolie Logan's aunt, near Dublin. One of Ellen's dresser drawers was stuffed with delicate underwear and nightgowns. Even the pillowcase on her bed had been made at the factory. There was no doubt that the linens were wonderful and would sell easily in a city where everyone was making good money. San Francisco had sprung back from the devastating earthquake, and it was now surging ahead, with even more buildings rising everywhere. Anyone who wanted to work, even women, could find a job.

But an ordinary job was not the same as a career, and neither of them was the same as owning a business that was very successful. It could happen. Imagine becoming rich and independent, without marrying. Imagine having all the right friends and going all the right places, without being tied down too young to the responsibilities of a husband and an endless row of babies. But maybe it was too much to hope for. Certainly it was too much to hope for if you had spent so much of the money you had promised to contribute to the plan. What possessed me to do it? Ellen thought.

She snapped an elastic over the end of her night braid and leaned forward to study her face better. What was wrong with me? she wondered. Why didn't Aaron Schuster take me to his grandmother's for tea, as he said he would? Why didn't he invite me out to dinner with his friends?

His tagging along after work with her and the other dress models from his father's department store did not count as a real dinner engagement, and that bitter knowledge had brought many sleepless nights to Ellen.

Stupidly, she had spent half of her savings on clothes that he probably never would see. And what would Kate say when she found out? If she saw the silk dress from Paris that cost two months' wages, even with the store discount? And when she saw the coat with the fur collar, the one that caused Ma, a fur hater, to shudder in disgust?

Ellen groaned and shut her eyes. Stupid, stupid, stupid, she thought. I must have lost my mind. I promised to save and share the expenses of renting a shop with Kate. All I could think of was being accepted by Aaron's friends. Going to the holiday parties, the cotillions, the dinners. And then later, the vacations at Pebble Beach and Tahoe. And perhaps even sailing to Hawaii one day. But the real truth was . . . the real truth . . .

Someone rapped lightly on the door, and it opened before Ellen could speak. Mrs. Stackhouse, her gray frizzled hair tucked into a net, poked her head in. "Everything all right, dear? I thought I heard someone groan."

Ellen despised the old woman, whose son paid her rent six months in advance, probably to be rid of her. "I'm fine. Good night," Ellen said firmly.

Mrs. Stackhouse smiled, winked, and shut the door, leaving Ellen with the feeling that the dreadful woman knew something about her. Probably she had overheard Ellen breaking every feminine rule by telephoning Aaron's house once and leaving a message with a sassy maid. Humiliating. Why had she done it? He had not called back for two weeks, and even then he had not bothered to apologize for his casual neglect. *Why had she put herself in that position?*

She turned out the light and crawled into bed, hoping her mother did not want to talk when she came upstairs. Ellen needed to confess everything to somebody, but she was not so young and silly that she would choose her mother for her confidences. Everyone who knew Ma knew that she would not for one instant tolerate Ellen's ambition to be accepted by Aaron's friends. Ma despised the young people featured so frequently and prominently in the city's gossip columns. "Rich, lazy, trouble-making idlers!" she would fume, elbow-deep in hot dishwater or bending over the stove, and consequently, Ellen always thought, completely unreasonable—and not to be challenged.

Ellen could not confide in sturdy Kate, either. Kate was

younger but much wiser—apparently. No one would catch her throwing her money away on clothes to impress the Burlingame crowd.

Someone else rapped softly on the door, and it opened a crack. "Still awake, I hope?" Kate murmured.

Relieved, Ellen sat up. She might have screamed at another visit from Mrs. Stackhouse. "Come in, and turn on the light."

Kate, in her flannel nightgown and woolen robe, slipped in and handed Ellen a small package wrapped in red paper. "Here," she said. "Merry Christmas. I could have waited until tomorrow, but there's such a ruckus in the kitchen on Christmas morning."

"Your gift is on the pantry sideboard," Ellen said. "I'll run down and get it." She began to swing her feet out of the bed, but Kate held up a hand to stop her.

"Don't. We'll have the whole house up, and Hugh and Joe will be demanding theirs, and your mother will kill us all. I haven't forgotten the rule—Christmas mass first, then gifts. Now, open yours and tell me what you think."

Ellen tore away the paper and opened the small box. An ornate silver locket! Ellen lifted it to examine it better.

"Open it," Kate urged.

Ellen pried up the lid and exclaimed, "Oh!" Inside she had found two small photographs, one of her and her mother, the other of Hugh and young Joe. "Where did you get the photos?"

"From that one that you all had taken by the photographer across from the wharf. Remember that day? I brought it with me to Ireland, and coming home, after I found this locket in New York, I decided to put your family pictures in it. I thought that would be better than your wasting this lovely old locket on a collection of your boyfriends, since they change so often."

Kate laughed at her own joke and Ellen managed to smile. But she was glad that the locket held the pictures of herself and her family. Boyfriends—they weren't worth it. Especially Aaron, for whom she had wasted months of her life, as well as the money spent on those clothes! And she did not have a photo of him, anyway—not a real one. She only had the newspaper photographs she had snipped out after the household papers had been gathered up and stacked on the back porch.

She fastened the silver chain around her neck and looked in the mirror. "It's perfect, Kate. It's beautiful. Thank you so much."

"Silver looks good on you, Ellen," Kate said. "Now, good night. I'd better get out of here before your mother comes upstairs." She left soundlessly, and Ellen looked at herself again in the mirror. It was a beautiful locket, a much grander gift than the book she was giving Kate. She tucked it inside the high neck of her nightgown.

Moments later, her mother walked in. "The light still on? I thought you'd be asleep by now. Hugh and Joe came back downstairs, and I made sandwiches for them. Do you want one?" She seemed on the verge of going out of the bedroom again.

"No, no, Ma. I'm not hungry—I had too much cake. Let's just go to bed. Tomorrow is a big day, and I don't want Mrs. Stackhouse in here again. She's already paid me one visit."

"Oh, her," her mother said. "If I didn't need a regular boarder, I'd drown the woman." Then she launched into a long recital of the work that lay ahead of them, feeding a boardinghouse with eighteen guests on the most festive day of the year.

Ellen's jaw practically cracked with a huge yawn. "What did you think of Kate?" she asked, interrupting her mother.

Mrs. Flannery, turning out the light, said, "You'd think that more than seven months had gone by. She looks seven years older. The trip is hard, but Jolie's dying—that must have been terrible." Her bed creaked under her weight and she sighed. "Ah, well, we're born to suffer here and get our reward in heaven, if we're lucky, just like the holy martyrs."

Ellen blurted sudden laughter. "Ma, you're awful. Just about the time I think life really is terrible, you say something like that and it's so ridiculous that you make me laugh."

"Wait until you're my age, dearie," Ma said. "You won't think it's funny then."

Ellen turned over on her side and pulled the quilt up close to her chin. I'm done with misery and suffering, she thought. After this I'll concentrate on work and saving money and . . .

Saving money! What am I going to say to Kate?

Christmas morning was cold and dark, with rain drizzling down when they walked to church and a nasty wind blowing on their way home. The holiday festivities seemed forced and tawdry to Ellen. Kate was so happy to be home that Ellen felt ashamed not to share her joy. "Home" was the boardinghouse, shabby and drafty, crowded with people who did not always get along—or even pretend to get along. Someone was always coughing, someone always wanted more breakfast coffee when the pots were empty. The boarders scattered after the meal, most of them to go wherever they planned to spend the holiday. Some went to church and came back, hungry for lunch even though Christmas dinner would be early in the afternoon.

"I'll never get through this day, God save me," Mary Clare complained, shuffling back and forth in the kitchen in her slippers, which had been slit open to ease her bunions.

Ma, rushed and cranky, handed Ellen a pot of cooked potatoes and a wooden masher. "Don't stand around, Ellen," she said. "You, Joe, didn't I tell you ten times already to bring in coal for the fires?"

"I did!" Joe protested. He showed his filthy hands to prove it and then wiped them on his trousers. "Why can't Hugh do it? He's bigger."

"You're thirteen!" Ma cried. "My own father had a job and supported his family when he was your age. You can at least make sure the fires are built up. Now go out and sweep the front steps."

Joe left, rubbing his dirty hands through his hair, and Ellen longed to slap him. She pounded the potatoes as if they were all the rich women who had ever treated her badly when she was modeling gowns for them, and all Aaron's stuck-up relatives who no doubt were celebrating the day being waited on by hordes of servants in large rooms with polished floors and great bouquets of flowers.

Thalia Rutledge chose that moment to slip into the kitchen and stand in the doorway with her thin chapped hands clasped against her chest. What on earth was she wearing? The dress was a mile too big. Ellen decided that it must belong to her mother. And then she remembered that this was Christmas, and as far as she knew, the child had received no gifts nor any special remembrances from anyone at all.

She had to swallow hard before she could speak. "Is there something I can do for you, Thalia? I didn't see you at breakfast. Are you hungry?"

The girl shook her head, looked down, and then said, "When it's time for dinner—when it's time—would you let me take my plate upstairs to eat? If it's not too much trouble."

"But don't you want to sit at the side table with Joe and Hugh? I thought you liked that. And Kate is home now. You'll love her."

But Thalia shook her head again.

It's that awful dress, Ellen thought. She hasn't anything decent to wear. Her school dress is too short and that dreadful brown thing she wears on weekends . . . I won't have it! Somebody has to do something for her.

"I want you to sit between Kate and me," Ellen said firmly. "Kate's just home from Ireland and she had a terrible time, so she needs cheering up. I want you to talk to her—tell her about school and the pigeons you feed in the backyard. Tell her about the last book you got from the library. But now, would you please help us a little? You can put the bread out on the tables. I'd really appreciate it."

It was hard to read the girl's expression. She seldom smiled, but in spite of it, she looked almost pretty. It was her hair, Ellen decided, that wonderful, fine, blond hair that clung in wispy curls around her pale face. Ellen turned and picked up a plate of sliced bread and handed it to her. "You can start with this one. Mary Clare is cutting more for the other tables."

Thalia smiled! Heavens, had she only wanted to be included? That was such an easy thing, but it was something Ma never extended to her, even though most of the other boarders were asked to help out from time to time. Even now, Ma was frowning faintly at Ellen, who merely shrugged it off.

Kate came in, only to be sent out again by Ma, who told her to rest. Kate did not look particularly full of good cheer, either. However, she had a good excuse. She had just finished an exhausting trip.

Ellen never had such an excuse, since social disappointments could hardly be equated with what Kate had been through. The holiday had to be endured, because it meant so much to everyone else. But Ellen, hating her own foolishness, waited all day for the doorbell to ring and a respectful messenger to hand her the unexpected (but oh, how expected!) bouquet of flowers or small and tasteful gift delivered by special arrangement with one of the smart new shops—or even by Aaron himself. In spite of her best intentions, Ellen snatched at quick daydreams in which Aaron appeared at the door, his coat spattered with rain, his eyes bright with pleasure at seeing her. "I was on my way to my grandmother's. . . ." Or "I'm running late, but I couldn't let the day pass without seeing you. . . ." Or, "I'm sorry I haven't called. Until yesterday, I was in Portland on business for my dad. . . ."

But he had been in San Francisco, and the newspapers had dutifully reported his attendance at certain important Christmas parties and dances.

And Ellen had not been invited to any of them as his

guest—or anyone else's guest, for that matter—so the wonderful silk dress and the stylish coat hung in the closet, and she had wept angry and resentful tears more than once.

The interminable holiday dinner passed, the tedious evening wound to a close, and bedtime came again. Ellen decided to concentrate on being more responsible at the department store—and saving even more of her salary. But her mind wandered back to Aaron, and the long day that had brought no remembrance from him. Outside in the dark, the incorrigible McCarthy brothers talked loudly under the street lamp to Mary McFee from across the street. When at last they told Mary good night and slammed into the boardinghouse, all Ellen could do was sigh. Either of the McCarthys, Luke or Matt, could be her boyfriend any time she snapped her fingers.

Aaron! So glibly dishonest, but so good-looking and so charming that she forgave him everything, always. The neglect that would have earned the McCarthy brothers a haughty reprimand called forth only silence from Ellen, silence or hasty assurances that yes, she did understand how busy he was, and yes, she could see perfectly well that his saying he would take her to the follies had not constituted a promise, and so wasn't she the silly goose to have waited for him outside the theater until the last person had gone inside and the big doors were closed by the uniformed man who had watched her pityingly?

She turned over, sighing, and pulled her rosary from

under her pillow. Perhaps she should start going to mass every morning with Ma, Mary Clare, and Mrs. Stackhouse.

The week between Christmas and New Year's was difficult for Ellen. One would think that women had something better to do at that time of year than shop for clothes! But Schuster's was crowded every day, and Ellen changed from one gown to another quickly, and then forced a glorious smile as she walked, turned, and walked again in the showrooms.

And, she told herself, never mind that these women, young and old, never saw her face or cared anything about her. Never mind that she was nothing more to them than a seamstress's dress form. One day she would have those soft furs that they dropped so casually over the backs of chairs. She would have the pearls, the useless little kid shoes, the hats that almost called out "Paris!"

And she would have Aaron Schuster on his knees, begging her to marry him. She smiled to herself as she imagined herself telling him that they could only be good friends.

Chapter 3

KATE

1909

"Will you have more tea?" Mary Clare asked Kate.

Kate, sitting at one end of the kitchen table with yesterday's newspaper spread out before her, woke from her half doze. "What? No, thank you. But if there's still some coffee . . . I think I'd like that better."

There was coffee in the bottom of the big pot, and Mary Clare filled a clean cup for her.

"Since there's just us two in here," Mary Clare began. She sat down next to Kate and fussed with her apron, touched her hair, which was coming loose from its knot, and brushed again at her apron. "Since there's just the two of us," she began again.

Kate blinked to clear her head of the heavy feeling that resulted from another sleepless night. "Is something wrong?"

"I was going to ask you that," Mary Clare said. She leaned closer. "Everybody worries about you. But didn't you have a terrible time, there in Ireland, and don't you wish now that you had never crossed the sea?"

Kate sipped her coffee before she replied. "I'm glad I went," she said. "I loved seeing Ireland, and I loved meeting the women who worked in the factory. Everybody was so kind to me."

"But the rain and mud," the older woman said. "And seeing how poor everybody is. And finding a priest behind every bush."

Kate, startled into laughter, shook her head. "Is that why you left Ireland? The rain and the mud and the priests?"

"I hated being so poor," Mary Clare said. She got up, sighed, and said, "I'm still—well, not rich—but things are not bad here. Not hopeless."

Kate glanced up as the cook returned to the stove. If she had been in Mary Clare's position, she knew that *she* would feel hopeless. What did the woman have to look forward to except years of working in someone else's kitchen?

"Of course, I could have married," Mary Clare said as she lifted the lid on a pot, peered in suspiciously, and stirred the contents. "But I'm better off working for somebody—because can't I quit if I want to? Isn't that better than being stuck with a husband who maybe isn't all you thought he would be? Marriage isn't always what young girls hope it is—but don't you dare tell Mrs. Flannery I said that, or she'll have me going to confession twice over before she's satisfied."

Kate, astonished into silence, could only stare at the cook. How many women felt like that? she wondered. "Well," she said inadequately. Mary Clare did not seem to hear. She was busy pulling saucers of leftovers out of the cooler and sniffing them.

Mrs. Flannery came in then, loaded with shopping parcels, and she said, "Kate! Feeling better this morning? I like seeing a little color coming back in your face."

The preparations for lunch began. When Kate left the kitchen, no one seemed to notice, for both women were examining a large fish Mrs. Flannery had just purchased.

Outside in the hall, Thalia Rutledge disappeared quickly into the small room that had been set aside for the boarders' coats and umbrellas. Had the child been eavesdropping? Kate did not pursue her to find out. She climbed the stairs, too depressed to think.

She had not gone to see Dr. Logan between Christmas and New Year's, even though she had told herself that it would be the ideal time. She could have begun the visit by presenting him with a gift of Aunt Grace's Christmas cake, exchanged good wishes, and then left soon, somehow magically avoiding the wrenching description of Jolie's last days. But the more she considered this plan, the worse it seemed—contrived and shallow, even heartless. Wouldn't he still have wanted the details of his only child's last illness? Could she have expected only holiday greetings? Or an offer of money?

She had even tried to put Jolie's memory out of her mind during the holiday week, but that was not possible. In spite of the Flannery family celebration, which included any of the boarders willing to join in, Kate was haunted by the events in Ireland. Ellen, nervously excited by holiday parties, urged Kate to go out with her and the young McCarthy brothers, both eagerly courting Ellen. Kate had not expected much from Luke and Matt, but surely Ellen understood that she was still in mourning for her friend and employer. Those months with Jolie had been a tangle of hope and despair as the pale girl struggled to survive. Even now, Kate sometimes thought she could still hear Jolie calling her at night, struggling and groaning as she burned with fever, too weak to even sit up. But still, Kate had made a point, for her aunt's sake, of smiling during the various household celebrations.

The new young boarder, Thalia Rutledge, had provided distraction. At the time of their introduction, the girl had responded to Kate's "How do you do" with only silence and a sober nod. The next evening, Kate found her playing Solitaire in a corner of the parlor and she sat down at the card table with her.

"How long have you been living here?" Kate had asked. She had not really been interested, but she had done her best to sound that way, for the girl seemed shy and depressed. Who could blame her? According to Aunt Grace, she had not received so much as a Christmas card from her family. The parents were typical actors, Mrs. Flannery had barked once, irresponsible daydreamers whom Ellen had met during her fortunately brief employment in the wardrobe department of a theater.

"We've been here two months," Thalia had said without looking up from her cards. She carefully placed a red jack on a black queen.

"And your parents went to Los Angeles?" Kate asked.

Thalia nodded.

"Are they coming back soon?"

Thalia nodded again, eyes on the cards.

"Do you like school?"

"Yes," Thalia said. However, she shrugged, too, taking back thc yes, at least in part.

Kate had been too tired and discouraged to labor on with a conversation that the girl obviously did not want to have. Since then, she had greeted Thalia kindly each time she saw her, but she seldom received more than a nod in return. Ellen and Joe could bring a few words out of her, and sometimes Joe played cards with her, a complicated game he seemed to have invented himself and which involved his winning every hand. Kate knew, from hearing Mrs. Flannery talk to her aunt, that the rent had not been paid on the big room Thalia was using, and there had been no word from her parents. She would have to be shifted to a small room on the third floor, so that the large front room could be rented out. Otherwise, no one knew quite what to do about her. Mrs. Stackhouse suggested—with a smile—that Mrs. Flannery contact the orphanage.

Halfway through the first week of January, Kate, alone in her bedroom, took out the travel journal Peter had found in the snow outside the train. Less than half of it had been used. Was it right to read someone else's personal thoughts? No. But she was sick of her own life. Perhaps this man, whoever he was, had dealt with his experiences better than she had. Perhaps she could learn. Or at least be distracted.

She reread the first entry and then turned to the second.

On the train to Rochester: I hate to travel. I particularly hate train travel. While I might suffer the company of strangers for an hour or two, anything more is a particular kind of hell. Facial expressions, articles of clothing, personal habits—those things that merit little attention in ordinary times—become maddening in close quarters. The train heaves and sways, it rattles and shrieks. The air is thick with smells from unwashed bodies, soiled clothing, and the exhaled evidence of the last meals gobbled. Voices grate, and I hear snatches of conversations that irritate me. Boat travel is different. When one has too much company, one can walk about on the deck and watch the coast slip past. An ocean trip probably would be pleasant.

Kate stopped reading for a moment. What a cranky man, she thought. But had she not felt much the same way on the train? She caught herself smiling. However, he might not always find an ocean trip so nice. She went back to the journal.

Later. I reached Rochester, eager to leap out of the car—forgetting for a moment that an even longer journey is ahead of me. Frederick was waiting at the station and took me to his home, talking excitedly the whole time about his Erie Canal project. I am happy for him, but I need something shorter and asked him if he had planned anything for me. Of course he had—about the canal!—and he has promised to send it by the end of the year. I was happy to spend three days in his company and even take a short walk along his passion, that dismal canal. We crossed a bridge that I expected to collapse under us, but he did not notice. I was glad to live to return to his home and a warm meal.

On the next night, over dinner, he asked about Isabel. My heart did not stop, as I might have expected. Suddenly I decided to go to Chicago to see her. The next morning Frederick accompanied me while I dealt with the necessary ticket changes, all the while assuring me that one day it will be possible for people to move themselves from one side of the country to the other without so much fuss—in hot air balloons! He took me back to the station the following day and gave me six books from his own library and a flask of brandy.

But I am already regretting my change in plans. I need to go home.

Kate began to turn the page, but she closed the journal instead. Had she really wanted to come home? she wondered. She had been *sent* home by Jolie, her employer, and it had seemed to her then that she had no real choice. But could she not have found a way to stay? Had she not wanted to live in Ireland and make a life there?

Worse yet, why had she not been able to see that Jolie was lying about her condition? Oh, she should have refused to go!

No matter. Kate blinked away tears. She was back in San Francisco, and the last year was over, and she could not relive a single day.

Halfway through the next week, Kate called Dr. Logan's house and asked Mrs. Conner, his housekeeper, if she should make an appointment with Dr. Logan or just drop by the house one day in the middle of the morning.

"I don't want to disturb him," she said. "I don't know if he even wants to see me."

"Of course he wants to see you," Mrs. Conner said. "We heard that you were back. But he doesn't make appointments with anyone anymore. Just come around at ten tomorrow. He'll be up by then. I'll let him know that you'll be arriving." Mrs. Conner hesitated a moment, and then said, "It must have been terrible for you, Kate."

"I wasn't with her, you know. Jolie died right after I left. Her aunt sent a wireless to the ship." Kate swallowed hard, remembering the moment she learned of Jolie's death. It had been expected, but still, Kate had been stunned, unable to catch her breath. *So soon? But I just said good-bye!*

"She wrote about you in every letter she sent home," Mrs. Conner said. "She was so happy."

Kate, remembering Jolie's suffering, did not respond except to thank Mrs. Conner and assure her that she would be at the house the following day, promptly at ten.

The next morning, over breakfast in the boardinghouse kitchen, Ellen advised Kate not to go. At least, not yet. "You don't owe him an apology, and I can tell by the expression on your face that it's what you're planning to do."

Kate put her cold toast down—she had not been able to swallow a bite—and shook her head. "No, I wasn't going to apologize. Well, yes, I guess I was. After all, he hired me to take care of her."

"And she had plenty of doctors checking her, on the trip," Mrs. Flannery said. She took a platter of pancakes from Mary Clare and bumped open the swinging door to the dining room with her wide hip. "What could you have done that they did not do, I'd like to know?" she asked as she left the room.

Kate, leaning on her elbows, sighed. "I have to go see him," she said.

Aunt Grace said, "It's simple courtesy, and you'll carry it off perfectly. Don't you worry about a thing. And when you get back, we'll go out for lunch and then stop by a bookstore. My treat."

But the visit to Dr. Logan was more than simple courtesy, and Kate was ashamed of herself. Dr. Logan had promised to deposit money in the bank for her if she went to Ireland with Jolie. She had agreed to the plan, even though she had intended to abandon Jolie when they reached Ireland. But in the end, she could not do it. Jolie was so sick and dependent. And Kate had grown fond of her.

And then there was the lure of the money.

Dr. Logan had promised her enough to guarantee her future. Those had been his exact words. She had no idea of the sum he had had in mind, and, at the time, she had been too embarrassed to ask. Asking now, after Jolie's death, would be impossible. And probably he had no intention of giving her anything, under the circumstances.

She drank the last of her coffee, refused another cup, and went upstairs to dress, burdened with her thoughts that seemed to run in pointless circles. She had no idea how much money there might be, but surely there would be enough to help with renting space for a while. Or at least enough to buy more of the wonderful Irish linens. For months she hungered to know exactly what Dr. Logan had meant to put aside for her. At the same time, she was embarrassed by her own greed. He had promised her a future, and she must trust him.

Except—now everything was different. She could be grateful only for not having confided in Aunt Grace and Ellen, and unfairly raising their hopes.

As she dressed in a neat black jacket and skirt, she forced her thoughts to the amount of money she had saved and Ellen's assurance that she had matched it, penny for penny. It might be enough to rent a small shop—very small!—for three months. Aunt Grace, who had recently inherited a few hundred dollars from a friend, was contributing, too. They might manage modestly and still be a success, in spite of their collective misgivings.

So, Kate thought, arranging her thick red hair in a simple knot at the back of her head, I don't need to regret anything except the sad death of a girl I'd come to love. I won't be selfish and greedy. I won't think I've lost anything—because I haven't. At least, I didn't lose anything that was mine to begin with.

And nobody needs to know my secret. Kate looked at herself in the mirror and then glanced away.

But I'll always know, she thought unhappily. I almost abandoned Jolie in Ireland. I stayed because I pitied her—and for the money. If her father has forgotten about it, or doesn't think I deserve it, then I'll have no complaint.

She pinned a hat in place, looked around the small, cluttered room she shared with her aunt, and resigned herself to living there forever, just one more of San Francisco's working young women.

The Logan house was just as she remembered it, a fine white place sheltered on the south by several trees. The morning was cool, and rain was threatening. Kate wished she had worn a coat.

She rapped the doorknocker and suddenly remembered the first time she had stood there, when she had come to apply for the job as Jolie's companion. She had been so frightened! And now she was frightened again.

Stout, black-clad Mrs. Conner opened the door as before, and this time she held out her arms to embrace Kate. "Kate," she said. Her faded eyes swam with tears. "You're so thin! Have you been eating? You look ill."

"I'm still a little tired," Kate told her. She followed Mrs. Conner to the library and sat on one of the sofas flanking the cold fireplace. "I hope I'm not too early."

"You're exactly on time, as always," Mrs. Conner said. "I'll tell Dr. Logan you're here, and Joseph will bring tea in. I'll ask him to light the fire, too. I hadn't realized how depressing this room is. We never use it these days."

She left Kate alone, to remember unhappily the hours she and Jolie had spent here, reading. Was it only a year ago? It seemed like a lifetime.

Joseph, the Chinese cook, came in carrying a silver tray with tea and biscuits. He smiled, bowed, and finally said, "It is good to see you again, Kate."

"It's been a long time," Kate said. "How is Nephew?"

"I let him boil the water for the tea," Joseph said, and he bent to light the fire. "But he is not ready to make biscuits yet."

He passed Dr. Logan in the doorway. Mrs. Conner, standing behind the doctor, smiled at Kate and closed the library door, leaving the two of them alone.

He had grown old. Old! His beard was completely gray, and his hands trembled.

"Kate," he said soberly. "I hope you had a pleasant Christmas. It must have been wonderful, being home again."

She folded her hands tightly in her lap. Christmas probably had been terrible for him. "The Flannerys enjoy holidays," she said. "They . . . helped."

He leaned back and sighed. "I've had letters from Jolie's

doctors," he said. "I should not have sent her to Ireland. I see that now, when it's too late."

There was more of this. Kate sat in silence, willing herself not to cry. He had a right to express his grief—and even his guilt—to her, and she would have to bear it. After all, Kate thought, in this life we owe people our attention. She had learned a great deal from the year and a half she had worked as Jolie's companion, and the most important lesson had been the value of listening.

Mrs. Conner brought in hot water and left again. Kate could hear boat horns on the Bay, and without looking at the windows, she knew that fog was gathering again. Nearby, a streetcar clattered past. A dog barked. Kate fixed her mind on Dr. Logan's voice, his recitation of regret. Once he stopped to cough, sipped tea, coughed again, and went on.

"Are you interested in nursing, Kate?" he asked suddenly, surprising her.

"No," she blurted. Then seeing the disappointment on his face, she added, "Once I had wanted to be a teacher. But never a nurse. I always would be too personally involved—too hurt—by things that can happen to patients."

"I could help you, you know, if you wanted to study nursing," he said.

She knew that, but she wanted her own shop. Nurses' salaries, like teachers', were disgracefully low.

Dr. Logan seemed to be waiting for her to add something to what she had said, and she had to stop herself from wringing her hands. This meeting was terrible—more painful than in her worst nightmares.

He put his cup and saucer down on the low table and leaned back. For a moment, he closed his eyes. Then he sighed and sat up straight. "I remember my promise to you, Kate. I deposited money in the bank for you before you left—I was sure I could trust you. We'll go over to Market Street now, and I'll let my banker explain everything to you."

She bent her head and blinked. Oh, thank God. He was going to help!

Their business took less than half an hour. Mr. Burleigh, the banker, took them into his office and explained to Kate that she would be allowed to draw as much or as little as she liked from the sum deposited for her, because it was hers, to do with as she chose. He took a sheet of paper out of a folder and pushed it across the desk to her, asking her to sign it, acknowledging receipt of the money. She signed without reading what was written on the paper. Dr. Logan was looking out the window, apparently thinking of something else.

Mr. Burleigh then pushed a small blue leatherette bankbook across the desk to Kate and spoke to her about interest rates. Her ears were ringing. She considered opening the bankbook to look at the figures and then changed her mind. She put it in her pocketbook and then, unsure of what to do next, got to her feet. Mr. Burleigh rose, too, and then Dr. Logan lurched to his feet, sighing.

"Thank you," Kate said. Her voice was hoarse.

"You're welcome to come back," Mr. Burleigh said, his voice kind for the first time. "It's quite a bit of money for a young girl. You may want—and need—advice."

"I'm sure I will," Kate said. "Thank you." She wanted out of the dark, stuffy office as quickly as possible, but the situation was so different, so strange, that she did not know how to manage it.

"Dr. Logan and I are going to the club," Mr. Burleigh said, perhaps sensing her awkwardness. "May we escort you somewhere first?"

They moved toward the door, and Kate struggled with the unprofessional desire to rush out of the room, across the new marble floor of the bank, out into the raw, foggy afternoon, and all the way home. But she walked with them and said her good-byes at the big door. Afterward, she would not be able to remember what she had said.

On the cable car going home, she took out the small blue book and looked at the amount of money Dr. Logan had given her, looked again, and put the book back. It was not as much as she had daydreamed about during the long afternoons while she waited for Jolie to awake from a restless nap, but it was more than logic had told her she would get—if she got any at all. She and Aunt would be able to have their own small flat now, because she had enough for several years' rent. And enough for a small shop, too, for a while at least. If it did not cost too much.

Or she could be daring and go back to school, and graduate from college as a teacher. Her original dream still might be realized.

But she was responsible for Aunt, and there was no way she could take care of her on the salary of a female teacher.

I shall have the shop, she thought. With Ellen's savings added to mine, there will be enough to stock the place for months. I hope. The rent is now assured!

When she reached the boardinghouse, Kate discovered that Mrs. Flannery and Aunt Grace had gone out for a while. Kate was eager to tell Aunt Grace about the money and what it would mean to them. The elderly woman found a certain amount of pleasure in living in the boardinghouse, but sometimes she told Kate she missed having her own kitchen and parlor. Now she would have them. The two of them would find a perfect small flat somewhere. Hugh could help! The construction company he worked for not only put up office buildings but also apartment houses. Hugh might know of a nice new place for rent. And if he did not, well then, his friends might. Or she and Aunt Grace would find one on their own.

And she would be looking for a small shop, too! Yes, she was glad to be home now.

Impulsively, she went up to the third floor, where she was storing the wicker trunks she had sent home from Ireland. They were full of linens of all kinds, beautiful tablecloths and napkins, underwear and petticoats, sheets and pillowcases, and delicate handkerchiefs. She sat back on her heels and looked at her treasures. The fabric was beautiful, and it still smelled of the lavender she had tucked inside when she packed it in Ireland.

Now the shop was becoming a reality.

She closed the trunks and left. Across the hall, the door was ajar on a small bedroom that Ellen used for a sewing room. But the sewing machine was gone, along with the dress form and all of Ellen's supplies. Instead, the place was furnished with a narrow bed, a dresser, and a table set up to be used as a desk.

The too-large dress Thalia had worn on Christmas was hanging from a peg under the sloped ceiling. This was her new room.

The single window overlooked the neighbor's roof. It was the most dismal spot in the entire house, up here across from the storage attic, and consequently impossible to rent. Poor Thalia. Poverty was hard, but being poor while only a child—and alone!—was terrible.

Life is unfair, Kate thought, feeling guilty for all of her good fortune.

A few minutes later, Aunt Grace returned, and as she promised, she took Kate out to lunch. Quietly, over the meal, Kate told her aunt about Dr. Logan's gift.

Chapter 4

ELLEN

On her best days, Ellen thought of herself as poised on the edge of great good fortune. She believed that if she wished on a falling star, the wish would come true—if not promptly, then in good time. And when Mary Clare told her fortune in tea leaves, Ellen was sure that she would receive money in the mail and meet interesting strangers before the week was out.

But sometimes Ellen thought of her life as a string of hopeless, and mostly silent, rebellions, interrupted occasionally with knots of total despair. Then the crowded boardinghouse, with footsteps echoing up and down the stairs, bursts of laughter, furious door-slamming quarrels, food smells, and endless boring conversations seemed more burdensome than ever. How could Ma be satisfied with this? Had she never wanted beautiful surroundings, theater tickets, new clothes, and—best of all—peace and quiet?

"Why do we rent to so many men?" she demanded of

her mother after breakfast one morning, when Matt McCarthy had fallen into a noisy argument about unions with the pompous insurance salesman who lived down the hall from him.

"Men have got money to pay the rent," Ma said. "Except for that Rutledge fellow, but then, he's an *actor,* so what could I expect?"

"Ma, don't start on the Rutledges again," Ellen begged. "It's not my fault that they didn't send the money for their room."

"And now I've got their girl living for free in the sewing room!" fumed Ma as she poured applesauce from a pan to a bowl. "Who knows how this can end?"

Ellen, on the verge of saying that she would pay the girl's rent out of her own salary, remained silent, remembering that she had to save extra money now, to make up for what she had squandered while wanting to please that wretched Aaron Schuster.

Clearly (on that particular day) life was hopeless, and anybody who thought otherwise had to have been born rich—and a man. Trust Irish women to know what life was truly all about. Standing side by side with Mary Clare, scraping plates into a bin, she wondered bitterly what the king of England was doing at that moment. Not scraping plates!

Kate's return to San Francisco had prompted such a hurricane of uncertainty in Ellen—uncertainty mixed with guilt—that Ellen had eaten herself into several unwanted pounds over the holidays, and now her waist measured a sickening twenty-one inches, enough to prompt Miss Franchone, her unfriendly supervisor at the department store, to ask her that very morning if she was "in a delicate condition" and then lift a skeptical penciled eyebrow when Ellen cried an indignant, "No!" at the idea that she might be pregnant. What nerve! How terrible! This was the worst insult that horrible woman had delivered yet!

After that, the day dragged even more than usual. The women who came to see gowns were unusually critical, causing Ellen to wonder if they managed to make themselves feel better about their bulges and wrinkles by ridiculing her. The dressing room smelled strongly of fabric dye, cheap dusting powder, and the damp plaster surrounding a leak in the ceiling. The wire in the high collar of one dress dug under Ellen's ear so hard that it brought tears to her eyes. The mark it left showed over the collar of the next dress, and a fat pockmarked matron snickered to her friend that "the little model shouldn't let her boyfriend kiss her on her neck." Ellen, nearly on tiptoes from pure rage, whipped her skirts around and left the room. The women laughed—and neither of them bought anything. Miss Franchone blamed Ellen, of course.

She left for home that afternoon in such a state of nerves that she walked rather than take the streetcar, hoping that the exercise would work off her anger. It did not, and so she spent the next hours in the boardinghouse under the scrutiny of her mother, snapping "Nothing!" every time her mother asked her what was wrong.

That night, Ma, exasperated with Ellen's sighing, sat up on her narrow bed and said, "For heaven's sake, either tell me what is wrong with you or go tell Father Sullivan, because I can't stay awake all night again, listening to you sigh and imagining the worst."

Ellen sat up and punched her pillow into a more agreeable shape. "I won't ask what the 'worst' is, and I can promise you that Father Sullivan wouldn't be sympathetic. He thinks girls shouldn't want anything except marriage, and I want all kinds of other things."

"Marriage isn't such a terrible life," Ma said, sighing herself now. They had had this discussion before. Ma understood—but somehow she did *not* understand—Ellen's need for independence.

"I don't want to get married!" Ellen said, loud enough to be heard in the adjoining rooms. "I don't want to have a baby every nine months and ten minutes."

"Well." Ma said, resigned. "*That* outburst must have entertained Mrs. Stackhouse and the rest of the boarders."

"Just so they know," Ellen said defiantly. She flopped down on the bed again and willed herself to mind her tongue. But she could not. "Ma," she exclaimed, sitting up again, "I want what other girls have. Wonderful clothes and parties and trips, at least for a few years, before I have to settle down to slave in a kitchen for the rest of my life!"

"What girls are you talking about?" Ma asked. "Those snobs you show off dresses to? Why don't you find a job that doesn't leave you so jealous? Because that's all that's wrong with you. Jealousy. And that's a sin you can take to Father Sullivan."

"I despise that man," Ellen said.

"You haven't been near mass for a year, except for Christmas!" Ma complained. "Maybe he's mellowed."

"Oh yes, I'm sure," Ellen said sarcastically. "He gripes about the unions more than he talks about God. Who wants to listen to that?"

Ma sighed. "Now you sound like Hugh. Don't you be so eager to speak well of unions! What's going to become of my children? Only Joe goes to mass regularly now, and I have to drag him. Not that it does him any good at all, for all the trouble he's in at school and around the neighborhood."

Ellen lay back down. "Go to sleep, Ma. And don't worry. We'll all survive."

But she lay awake for hours, wondering what the coming year would be like. Soon she would have to talk to Kate about money and their plans for a shop. Soon.

~

Morning came too early, and with it, another day at Schuster's, San Francisco's finest department store. Ellen and the several other pretty young women who modeled the gowns were always under close inspection by the universally detested Miss Franchone, who was called "Frankie" behind her back, and any variation in weight brought down storms of abuse, most of it in the hearing of the other models. Ellen's extra pounds came up for discussion again that morning, at the top of the stairs outside the dressing room door, even before she had removed her hat.

Ellen, her face so scarlet that she felt as if her skin might split, raised her chin and said, "I'll thank you not to dare to speak to me that way again."

Miss Franchone turned her skinny back haughtily, but she did not say anything more. Ellen was certain that she must have heard the rumors that Ellen was admired by Aaron Schuster, the younger son of the store president—and so she felt quite confident that she could walk off and slam the dressing room door, leaving the dreadful hag huffing impotently behind her. But still—still—it was horrible that this ugly, dry stick of a woman should speak to her so. And Ellen hated herself for the midnight indulgences of cookies and candy all through the holiday season. Oh, she *was* getting fat! And then what? Soon she would look like Ma.

Lucy, the dresser, looked up when Ellen banged the

dressing room door behind her. "You're almost late," she said, without a trace of scolding in her voice. The small woman was badly crippled, with a clubfoot and crooked spine, but her skills in altering clothing were superb, and all the models loved her. She took a dress off a pole rack and held it out. "Two customers are here already."

Ellen began unhooking the dress she wore. "Did Miss Bridely tell you they were *really* here? I hate getting ready for people who are going to be an hour late." Miss Bridely was the head saleswoman.

"They're on time," Lucy said as she held out the dress Ellen was to model. "They aren't anybody, and the nobodies are always on time. It's the other ones who make us wait."

Ellen laughed, stopped abruptly, and bit her lip. "Isn't that the truth?" she asked bitterly. "Who are they?"

"Two women from New York, Bridely said. One is getting married, and her husband-to-be is treating her to any dress she wants for her wedding trip."

Ellen, busy fastening the belt to hide the joining of the dress's top and skirt, smiled. "Well, this silk taffeta is impractical enough to satisfy anyone. Oh, heavens! The belt won't close."

"All those molasses cookies," Lucy said. Her small, crooked hands were surprisingly strong, and she yanked the ends of the belt together and hooked them. "There. Just don't laugh and pop it open."

"I never laugh when I'm showing a dress," Ellen said. "Where are Germaine and Betty?"

"The Castles and Fairchilds are here, in the Rose Room," Lucy said. She pulled a pair of pale blue shoes from a large drawer and bent down to replace Ellen's street shoes with the delicate and useless ones that matched the dress. "These will hurt," she warned.

Ellen studied herself in the three-way mirror that revealed everything, and she touched her smooth hair approvingly. "The Castles and Fairchilds?" she said. "Two fat mothers with three fat daughters between them, all fanning themselves with their cotillion cards, and I don't care, I don't care, I don't care." She snickered and thought of the hopelessness of their watching slender Germaine and barely rounded Betty mincing back and forth in ball gowns that cost more than the models made in the entire year. No matter how the gowns were altered, the overstuffed daughters would still end San Francisco's social season without husbands. There were too many beautiful and wealthy young women available, and too few wealthy men interested in finding mates. And why should they? Didn't men have all the say in who married and who did not? And what was their hurry? They didn't need to concern themselves about finding a way to feed themselves. Women had to find husbands or be old maids. And the old maids who weren't wealthy must work at menial jobs. If they were not lucky enough to have their own businesses.

Bridely, a tall woman with lusterless, dyed black hair, stuck her head in the door. "Ellen! To the small showroom." The door clicked shut.

The small showroom was for ordinary women, who waited for the models and sipped tea served by maids in black dresses with white aprons and neat little caps. Palm trees bent over velvet sofas. Silk draperies hid the outside world. The carpet was only slightly thinner than the carpet in the elegant Rose Room, where the furniture was upholstered in silk brocade. Ellen was prepared to see two anxious young women waiting, unaccustomed to splendor and showing it with every gesture.

She was not disappointed. They sat stiffly side by side, and Bridely introduced the Misses Carson and Jones quickly, then stood back, explaining the virtues of the dress Ellen wore as she paraded back and forth, smiling.

The young women looked stupefied. "I don't know . . ." the bride-to-be said as she watched Ellen.

"You don't have to decide now," the other said, but she sounded doubtful.

"We have several other gowns to show you," Bridely said. The young women seemed surprised. Ellen pitied them and gave them her brightest smile.

"When did you arrive in San Francisco?" Bridely asked the young women as Ellen whisked out, to be helped into another gown by Lucy.

"Late on Christmas Eve," one of them said, as the door

closed behind Ellen. "I never want to see another train."

They must have been on the same train as Kate, Ellen thought. I'll ask her as soon as I get home.

Kate. A small, nasty headache settled behind Ellen's eyes. She would have to talk to Kate about money soon, and face the disappointment she would see on her friend's face.

But the world changed in an instant, when Lucy handed Ellen a small box and an envelope when she entered the dressing room. "A messenger brought these for you," she said.

Aaron's handwriting was unmistakable. Ellen ripped open the envelope as Lucy unhooked her dress. "I'm back in town," the note read, "and eager to see you. Sorry about the late Christmas gift, but you know how I mean it. Yours always, Aaron."

Ellen could have cried with delight, but Lucy, who knew everything—or at least guessed everything—must not be given information that did not suit Ellen's purposes, so she put the note and the small package in the pocket of her coat, hanging in the corner. But she no longer minded the exasperating business of unhooking and hooking, and a small disaster with her hair as the tall collar snagged it out of place, and another pair of shoes two sizes too small. She no longer cared about her small salary—and her small bank account. She might be going out to dinner this very evening—and meeting Aaron's grandmother this weekend.

So whatever was in the box could wait until she was home and safely in her room and could gloat in peace about the possibilities.

And he had been out of town? That explained everything. Ellen chose not to remember that she had read his name several times in the society columns of the papers over the holidays.

The bride-to-be bought the stylish black-and-white-striped gown with the clever bolero jacket in daring yellow velvet. Bridely thanked them, and they thanked Ellen. But she barely heard them. Her job had a certain glamour—and owning her own shop could be even more glamorous, depending on what she and Kate sold. There would be room for her in Aaron's set of friends. And in a few years, when she had tasted all that the privileged life in San Francisco might offer, she could settle down.

Even though Aaron did not contact her during the long day, she was still certain that she would see him that evening. Her ecstatic mood lasted until the store's closing, when Kate met her as she left by the employees' door on the south side of the store. She almost did not see Kate at first, for she wanted nothing more than to hurry home and wait for Aaron's call, but Kate grabbed her arm, laughing, and said, "What streetcar are you chasing?"

Ellen, wildly aware of the small package in her pocket, laughed, too, and said, "What brings you downtown? I thought you hated it this time of day?"

"I'd better get used to it," Kate said. "Look, do you have time for coffee before we go home? I have something to talk about before we get back to the boardinghouse."

Ellen's heart sank. She wants to talk about her—our!—idea for a shop, she thought, despairing. And now I have to tell her about the money. And to make matters worse, Ellen was wearing the coat with the fur collar, the coat that had cost her so much money that she had invented the lie she would tell her mother even before she had bought it. A used coat from one of the customers, sold at half price? Her mother, who knew nothing about what went on behind the scenes at Schuster's, believed her, or at least Ellen had thought that she did. Ellen knew of no customer who would offer a coat at half price to anyone, thereby admitting that she needed money. But in the Flannerys' world, people sold things they did not need or could not afford to keep. So why not?

The fur collar seemed to choke her now, and Kate did not comment on it.

"I promised Ma that I'd help with dinner," she said feebly.

"I won't keep you more than ten minutes," Kate said joyously. "I have wonderful news."

So Ellen went with her to the small café a block away. Fortunately, she remembered the two young women who had come in to shop that morning—even their names, thank goodness!—and so she asked Kate if she knew them. Anything to delay the conversation about money.

"Miss Jones and Miss Carson? That must be Edith Jones and Adele Carson. I talked to them often on the train. We exchanged addresses—and I had intended inviting them for lunch soon—but this is a wonderful coincidence. Look, we can go out to tea with them some Sunday. Would you like that? We'll go to one of the nice hotels and give them a great treat."

They sat at a small, newly washed table while a young man with scarred skin served them coffee in thick cups. "I'll see," Ellen said numbly. At that moment she would have considered anything.

Then Kate's reason for meeting her could no longer be avoided. She listened in amazement while Kate told her a tale of a promise of money, if she went to Ireland with Jolie. "It's enough for me to move Aunt Grace and me into a small apartment somewhere—and to open a shop. I can do both! And what we've saved between us can stock the shop so well that we're sure to be a success. Think of it! Everything we planned is coming true—and even more."

It was almost too much news for Ellen to absorb at once. Money? Kate had been given money for accompanying Jolie to Ireland? For one quick instant, Ellen remembered that the job of companion to the sick girl could have been hers, but then she dismissed that and settled with horror on the realization that Kate would now expect her to tell how much money she had saved. Stock the shop?

With more than the linens Kate had sent from Ireland, naturally. Much more.

Costing much more money.

"Let's go home," Kate said, finishing her coffee and getting to her feet. "But not a word to anyone. Aunt Grace knows, because I want to start looking for a flat right away. But I don't want others to know that we have enough to open a shop so easily, because I don't want anyone begging for a loan. You know how the boarders are. I'll be talked out of it in a week, if the McCarthy boys find out about it. They're dying to own an automobile. And somebody always has a sad tale to tell. I know I sound selfish, but this is for us, Ellen, for our own shop and our own independence. And for my aunt. Do you agree?"

Ellen nodded, unable to keep the smile off her face. Oh yes, this could mean independence. And she would find a way to tell Kate that she had let her down about the savings—but she would make things right. There would be ways she could do it, by working longer hours and taking more responsibility. Oh yes, this could work out, without Kate's disapproval.

But she would have to find the right time to tell her.

They reached home as Hugh and the McCarthy brothers arrived, grimy and high-spirited. Joe was repairing his old bicycle on the front porch, something that would have earned him a loud scolding from Ma, and the McCarthys obviously were torn between the charms of Ellen and the fascination with the slipped chain.

Ellen solved their predicament. "Leave me alone!" she said crisply as she swept through the door.

She was a woman of property. Almost.

Someday she might even be able to move out of the boardinghouse.

Late that night, before Ma came upstairs to bed, Ellen opened her gift. Inside the small box lay a circle pin of pearls and gold. It was discreet, in perfect taste, but valuable enough to infuriate Ma if she saw it. Reluctantly, Ellen hid it at the bottom of one of her drawers. It proved that Aaron cared about her—even if he had not sent a message that he had wanted to see her that evening. Maybe tomorrow . . .

She lay awake most of the night planning her thank-you note.

Chapter 5
KATE

"So what do you think, Kate?" Hugh Flannery asked, one Sunday afternoon in February.

Once more, Kate looked around the living room of the second-floor flat, unable to stop smiling. "It's wonderful," she said. "I love the smell of new wood and paint. And all the light coming in! And two bedrooms! This would be perfect for Aunt Grace and me."

The building had just been completed—Hugh knew some of the carpenters and had told Kate about it as soon as the flats became available for rent—and it was located within a comfortable walk from shops and restaurants, which would suit Aunt. The bay windows in the living room and dining room overlooked a pleasant street, and the windows in both bedrooms offered a tiny spangled glimpse of San Francisco Bay. It was expensive, but what was not expensive here, where hundreds of people were still living in the temporary shelters put up in the parks? "I can afford this," Kate said, as much to herself as to Hugh.

"All the stairs won't bother your aunt?" Hugh asked. Kate thought that he sounded almost hopeful. While he had agreed to help Kate find an apartment, he had not been enthusiastic about her moving out of the boardinghouse. And his mother was expressing her own disappointment at every meal. But Kate had promised Aunt Grace that they would find their own place as soon as they could, and Kate had wanted this independence, too. It would be the first step in their new life.

"She is much better now than she was," Kate said. "Remember, she's been climbing the steps in the boardinghouse. After she was hurt, we were afraid she'd always need crutches, but now she says she's ready to dance."

Hugh, tall and thin, leaned against a windowsill and looked out. He was silent for a long moment and then he said, "The quake seems like a whole lifetime ago. Sometimes I forget how bad things were afterward. Now, so much has changed."

Kate joined him at the window. "You like helping to rebuild the city, don't you?"

He did not smile. "I like it, yes. Most of all, I like helping with the planning of the new buildings. I like to be able to see into the future of a building site."

"You're not like the McCarthy boys," she said. "They like payday best."

Hugh laughed. "They're all right. They liven up a crew, and I don't mind being on a job with them. They're excited about unions now, talking big and going to meetings every week." He stopped and looked out the window again. "So, Kate, what will you say to the landlord when he comes back? There are only two flats left in the building. Much as I hate to say it, if you don't decide today to take one, tomorrow probably will be too late."

"I shouldn't make the decision without Aunt Grace. . . ."

"It's your money, Kate," he said soberly.

She had told him about Dr. Logan's gift, and she had asked him to keep it secret. "You haven't said anything?" she asked now, needing reassurance. "I don't want anybody twisting my arm for a loan. I need every cent, for the flat and the shop—and all the things Ellen and I will need to buy."

Hugh looked uncomfortable. "No, I didn't tell. But Kate, wasn't Ellen supposed to help out with the costs? Isn't that the promise she made you?"

Kate now knew that Ellen had not been able to save as much as she had planned, and Ellen's confession had left her disappointed—but she had not complained. Still, she was not sure how to handle the business arrangements. They had planned to be partners, but Kate was practical enough to realize that she should not make Ellen a full partner when she was contributing less than a quarter of the money. She needed advice, but Hugh was not the right person to give it. He knew nothing of money management. She would go back to the bank and talk to Mr. Burleigh.

"Ellen and I will work out everything about the shop," Kate said firmly. "You said you would ask around for us. I hate to keep bothering you, but you know the city better than anyone."

Hugh shrugged. "Better than some," he said. "But small places—Kate, they're awfully expensive to rent. The minute one opens up, there's a line of people with their hands full of money. Everybody wants to start up a business in San Francisco now."

Kate turned around once more to look at the flat. "The first thing is for Aunt and me to get settled. Then I can start seriously looking for a shop." She smiled up at her friend. "Maybe I need a rental agent."

"No, don't do that," Hugh objected. "There are too many crooks around. I'll find something. And the McCarthy boys can keep their eyes open, too. They know plenty of people. And they'd do anything for my sister."

The landlord came in then, blustering a little, pushing for an answer, warning her that he had a long list of potential tenants and had only agreed to show her this place as a favor to Hugh. Kate assured him that she and her aunt wanted it, and they settled the details in his ground-floor flat, while his stout wife started his Sunday dinner in her new kitchen.

"Now all I need is furniture—and some strong people

to help me move it in," Kate said as she went downstairs to the street with Hugh.

"I don't want to go furniture shopping with you!" Hugh said, alarmed. "But if you need help with moving, count on me. And the McCarthys, too."

As they walked toward Market Street, Kate looked back at the building that would be her home soon. Sometimes it seemed to her that she had never left San Francisco for Ireland. Now if only she finally could forget the earthquake.

"Did you ever notice that people don't talk about the quake?" she asked Hugh.

He quickened his pace, and she nearly had to run to keep up. "Nobody talks about it because nobody can bear remembering it," he said. "And neither can I. Those were the worst days of my life, of all our lives."

Kate kept up with him silently. He was right, of course. Who wanted to think about the awful days when homeless people wandered in the ashes, searching for food and water? They had been among them, children who had grown up in a few terrible hours. But wise people did not look back over their shoulders.

"But there is something I want to talk about," Hugh said. "Ellen and that Schuster fellow. I've asked her what's going on, but she tells me to mind my own business."

"Well, nothing *is* going on," Kate said. "As far as I know, she hasn't seen him since the holidays, and I read in the paper a couple of weeks ago that he and some of his friends were going to Hawaii. But I didn't say anything to Ellen. Hawaii! He thinks nothing of taking trips like that, and here I am, grateful that I have the means to pay the rent. I'm like your mother, Hugh—I don't know what Ellen sees in that crowd."

"She ought to settle down and get married," Hugh said gruffly.

"Hugh!" Kate cried. "Can you picture her cooking meals and canning pears and begging a husband for pin money? You know she doesn't want that!"

"And neither do you, right?" he asked, looking straight ahead.

"Well, would *you*?" Kate asked angrily. "Why should we be any different? We want work—and our own security."

"Ma worries about her," he said. "She's got no father, and with only Joe and me to watch out for her—and there's that Schuster fellow. . . . " His voice trailed away with a growl.

"I see Joe watching out for her!" Kate scoffed, smiling. She was anxious to get Hugh off the subject of his sister. And Aaron Schuster. No one worried about Ellen more than Kate, but Ellen would answer no questions and seemed to be getting along better now than she had been when Kate first returned home.

Two blocks from the apartment house, Kate noticed

the street sign and stopped in her tracks. "Hugh, do you want to pay a Sunday call with me?"

Hugh gawked at her. "Call? On who? I hate that sort of thing. Is it somebody I know?"

"It's a young woman I met on the train coming out to California. She lives on this street with her grandparents. In fact, she must live in that house over there. The one with the pretty little iron gate."

"Aw . . . " Hugh groaned.

"You'll like her. Come on, let's go see if they are home."

Adele Carson answered Kate's knock and smiled when she saw her. "I meant to telephone you a dozen times, but Grandma was ill and time just got away from me. I'm so glad to see you, Kate! Come in!"

Kate introduced Hugh to the pretty young woman and was satisfied to see Hugh blush. Good. Served him right to be attracted to somebody besides that awful McFee girl. Adele presented them to her grandparents, who were reading the Sunday papers, and soon they were having tea in the dining room, surrounded by half a dozen tall houseplants, a sassy parrot on a perch, and a small dog that jumped up into Hugh's lap and conquered him immediately. Kate did her best to keep a grin off her face.

Kate told Adele that the model for the dress Edith had bought was her good friend, who was also Hugh's sister. Adele was impressed. "She's so beautiful," she said. "Edith's never stopped talking about her—and those clothes! She'd go back and buy another dress in a minute, if she could afford it. But they're getting married next month, and neither of them can be extravagant now. What an exciting job your friend has! I'm going to start looking—but I don't want to go back to sewing shirtwaists again."

"Is that what you did in New York?" Hugh asked, with an interest that surprised Kate—until Hugh asked Adele if she had belonged to a union.

"No, more's the pity," Adele said briskly. "We might have been able to have forced the owners to leave the doors unlocked during the day. Someday there'll be a fire in one of those factories, and girls will be killed because they couldn't get out the doors. We wanted more than just money. We needed safety, too."

"Now, now," her grandfather chided. "Let's have no talk of unions when we have guests."

"I'm all for unions," Hugh said in a mild tone, and Kate stared at him. Usually any opposition to unions caused Hugh to argue angrily.

It did not take an idiot to see that Adele was now half in love with Hugh, even though she was older than he was. But Hugh was oblivious. So far.

Hugh talked about unions all the way home, but Kate barely listened. Adele envied Ellen her job, but Ellen hated it. She stayed only because she hated everything else even more. Yes, Ellen needed to work for herself. But money management was a problem. Kate would see Mr. Burleigh and ask his advice. If he could not help, then perhaps he knew someone who could. Kate could go no further without understanding business better than she did.

Sundays were often quiet in the boardinghouse. Hugh went to the kitchen because he was hungry and his mother would always fix him a sandwich or cut him a big slice of pie, no matter when he came in. Kate, climbing the stairs to her bedroom, was thinking of the shop and scarcely paying attention to anything around her. But she heard the dry scuttle of feet on bare stairs above her when she reached the second-floor landing, and she looked up, to see the quick flutter of a dark green skirt. Thalia, wearing the dress Ellen had cut down for her from one of her own.

Why is she avoiding me? Kate wondered. She paused on the landing, still looking up, and heard Thalia's door slam. She seems to dislike me for some reason, Kate thought uncomfortably. Strange, silent Thalia, back in school now at Ellen's insistence, while she waited—and waited—to hear from her parents in Los Angeles. Ridiculous people! From what Mrs. Flannery said, they had spoiled their son and turned their girl into a sullen little sneak and liar, two traits Mrs. Flannery despised. But what could happen to the girl, left on her own?

Goosebumps rose on Kate's arms, and she hugged herself. No matter. Thalia was safe enough in the boardinghouse, because Ellen was looking out for her, and Mrs. Flannery would not turn out a child, no matter how much she disliked her. Joe was good to her and played checkers with her nearly every night, even letting her win sometimes, an astonishing act of charity for the boy who grew wilder every week. Still, Kate could not explain the uneasy feelings that she had while she put away her hat and pocketbook. She should go down to the kitchen, where Aunt Grace probably was sitting in her accustomed chair and watching Mrs. Flannery and Mary Clare prepare dinner, and perhaps helping with peeling potatoes or rolling butter balls and dropping them into ice water. Aunt Grace would not be satisfied with only Hugh's description of the new flat.

But she wanted to run up to the third floor, too, and open the wicker trunks once more and look at the linens stored there, the things that would be sold in her shop. Just a quick look, she told herself, and then I'll go down to the kitchen.

Thalia's door, opposite the door to the storeroom, was shut, and Kate heard nothing going on behind it. She opened the storeroom—and stopped, clapping both hands over her mouth. The trunks were open, and the linen goods were scattered around in heaps, as if someone had been looking for something.

Or as if someone had been bent on making as big a mess as possible.

Oh, look at this! Kate knelt on a pile of pillowcases and picked up a delicate petticoat. The lace on the bottom had been ripped off. And here! Table napkins soiled as if someone had rubbed them on the dusty attic floor. And the embroidered nightgowns, with their tiny mother-of-pearl buttons torn off.

Kate rose shakily. Who could have done this?

She walked out into the hall and heard, from behind Thalia's door, stifled laughter.

"Thalia?" she called out. "Thalia, open the door."

Silence.

Kate knocked briskly, her anger growing.

Silence.

Kate tried the doorknob, but the door was locked. "Thalia!" she shouted, pounding on the door. "Did you do this? Did you?"

Inside the room, she heard the faint giggle again. Then, finally, the door was unlocked and it swung open. Thalia stood there, her face white. She saw the nightgown Kate held and said, "Somebody was up here. I heard footsteps, but I was afraid to come out. It must have been somebody very bad, and I was afraid." Large tears trembled in her eyes, broke, and streamed down her face. "I should have come out and looked, but I'm alone, and I *was* afraid."

Kate could have slapped her. She wanted to slap her! She knew she was lying, as surely as she had ever known anything. But she had no idea what to do at that moment, so she left Thalia's room and ran down the stairs to the kitchen.

"Look at this!" she cried, and she held out the nightgown for everyone to see.

"Whoa!" Hugh said, backing up. "I'd rather not, if you don't mind."

"Oh, Hugh, don't be such a donkey," his mother said. "Heavens, Kate, what happened? Look, all the buttons gone. And the lace torn nearly away from the hem. And see here, the pocket ripped right off!"

"Nearly everything is out of the trunks and scattered all over," Kate said, her voice shaking. "I haven't looked at every piece, but many things have been damaged."

"Thalia!" Mrs. Flannery cried, red-faced.

"That girl!" Mary Clare cried, shaking a potato masher. "I'll give her what for!"

"But we don't know it was her, do we?" Aunt Grace asked. "Kate? Do we?"

"I went to her room," Kate said slowly. "I thought I heard her laughing. . . . But she cried and said someone was up there. I suppose . . ."

The people in the kitchen looked at each other. "Well, who, then?" Mrs. Flannery demanded. "One of the boarders? Everybody goes in and out of the storeroom all the time. That's what it's there for. But nobody ever bothered anything that belonged to anyone else."

"Who would tear up that stuff you sent from Ireland?" Hugh asked. "Nobody cares except the women, and they carry on about it like it was holy altar cloths or something."

"Hugh Flannery, watch your mouth," his mother said. "No, but Kate, I'm quick enough to blame Thalia for just about anything—the girl gives me such a creepy feeling sometimes—but this is terrible. I can hardly believe it was her. I'll come up and have a good look."

"She must know you'd throw her out into the street if she did something like that!" Mary Clare said.

"She'd end up in the orphanage," Kate's aunt said. "Let's all go up and have a look."

"Mary Clare, pull those potatoes off the heat," Mrs. Flannery said, and she led the way up to the attic storeroom. They found Thalia there, gathering up the linens from the floor and folding them neatly. Her eyes were swollen from tears, which still dripped steadily down her face.

Mrs. Flannery snatched a petticoat away from Thalia. "I'd like an explanation of this, miss," she said.

Thalia made a helpless gesture. "I was sleeping after lunch. I've been so tired and sick since Mama and Papa left. And I thought I heard somebody open the storeroom door. And I thought I heard noises in here. But I was afraid, and I couldn't go look because I didn't know but maybe it might have been that friend of Papa's who was always so mean to me, and maybe he was looking for Papa's trunk that he was going to leave behind, except that he didn't after all, and—"

"What on earth are you talking about?" Mrs. Flannery demanded. "Are you saying that a stranger was here in my house, stealing from our Kate, and you didn't scream to warn us?"

"I was afraid," Thalia wept.

Aunt Grace stepped forward now and placed one hand on Thalia's shoulder. "Stop crying," she said. Thalia obediently wiped her eyes on the backs of her hands. "You say someone was here?" Aunt Grace asked.

"Looking for Papa's trunk!" Thalia declared. "I just know it. Papa was storing some of his things here, and he—"

"Rubbish!" Mrs. Flannery said.

"Rubbish!" Mary Clare echoed triumphantly.

Kate sighed. "Probably most of the linen can be fixed," she said. She was weary all over now. The happiness finding the right flat had brought had been erased by malice. "Hugh, when I finish putting the things back, will you carry the trunks down to my room? Aunt Grace and I will keep our door locked so that this 'mysterious man' can't go through them again."

"Then you don't blame me?" Thalia asked. Her eyes were an odd blue, so pale that they were almost colorless, and it seemed to Kate that they glittered with a cold hatred that was incomprehensible to her.

Oh, I blame you, all right, Kate thought wearily. But what good would it do? It might not take much more than this, after all, to convince Mrs. Flannery to put you into the orphanage, and you'd end up like the rest of those pathetic girls—a servant or sweatshop worker—or worse.

"Let Ellen sort it all out," she told Mrs. Flannery. "She knows Thalia best."

"She's wasting her pity," Mrs. Flannery said bitterly.

"Just let Ellen handle it." Kate looked sternly at Thalia then and added, "These things belong to Ellen, too, you know."

Thalia's mouth fell open. "I didn't know that."

Mary Clare pushed the girl roughly across the hall into her own room and banged the door after her, and the women set about repacking the wicker trunks, while they exclaimed over the damage.

"But there's nothing that can't be fixed by someone clever with a needle," Aunt Grace said. "I can fix most of these things, and Mary Clare is good with lace."

"I'll pay you," Kate said hastily to Mary Clare, who had enough to do working in the boardinghouse.

Mary Clare, examining the torn lace on a pillowcase, said, "I'd take one of the petticoats in exchange, if you're willing."

"Then everything is settled," Aunt Grace said briskly. She hated fusses of any kind, and, Kate told herself, they would be leaving the place soon enough—and out of Thalia's reach.

"Aunt!" Kate cried, suddenly remembering that her aunt did not know about the flat. "I found the perfect place for us. Hugh showed it to me. And I've told the landlord that we'll take it."

Aunt looked startled until Hugh said, "It wouldn't have lasted until tomorrow, Miss Keely."

Aunt admired Hugh so much that she accepted anything he said. "But whatever are we going to do for furniture?" she said. "We had nothing left after the fire."

"We'll start looking for things tomorrow," Kate told her. "There are sure to be bargains this time of year. And there are enough secondhand stores to keep us busy until we're ready to move in. And Hugh and his friends will help us."

"Oh, sure," Hugh said.

"I hate to see you go!" mourned Mrs. Flannery.

"But we'll be close enough for Aunt Grace to walk over and have coffee with you," Kate said, anxious to reassure both older women.

"I trust you, Kate," Aunt said suddenly. "I trust you for everything."

There was a quiet moment in the disheveled room while all the women looked at her. Then Kate said gruffly, "Well, Aunt, we've been through a lot."

"God bless us, that's the truth," Mrs. Flannery said.

"Aw, are we all going to cry over old times?" Hugh demanded. "I for one don't want to remember anything that happened further back than yesterday."

"There speaks the mouthpiece of the saints," his mother said wryly.

So they all laughed, then, the painful moment past, and by the time Ellen came home from her afternoon with friends, the wicker trunks had been stacked in the room Kate shared with her aunt, Hugh had taken off for a ride in the automobile the McCarthy boys had borrowed, and Thalia was setting the dining room tables meekly, her reddened eyes cast down.

After Ellen heard the events of the afternoon, Kate watched her murmuring to Thalia in a corner of the dining room, smoothing back the girl's wavy hair, and finally hugging her with more kindness than Kate could have managed.

"Kate will forgive you," Kate heard Ellen say. "I'm sure of it."

I'm not so sure about that, Kate thought. She had seen Thalia's pale, triumphant stare over Ellen's shoulder.

How strange that Ellen did not want to have her own children, since she was so good with them. Gruff sometimes, like her mother, but always good. More than once she had charmed the children of a wealthy woman so much that the woman had bought a gown in gratitude.

But Kate could not bring herself to speak to Thalia for several days, and whenever Thalia saw her glancing in her direction, she smirked. Kate made sure her bedroom door was locked whenever she and her aunt were not in it.

One night she read another entry in the stranger's travel journal.

The wind is cruel and cold in Chicago. I found a hotel sheltered on a side street, but the wind caught me out and howled outside my window all night. I could not sleep, for many reasons.

I went to Isabel's house and learned from her parents' maid that she was in the hospital with a badly wrenched back. Her family was not at home. I hurried to the hospital, only to be turned away by her father, who blamed Jeffrey for what he calls Isabel's "recklessness." Without his permission, she had bought a poorly broken horse and was thrown, something he said would not have happened had she never met my "wild" brother. Isabel, according to the furious old man, had been a perfect daughter until Jeffrey entered her life. I held my temper and did not remind him that I had known Isabel long before Jeffrey had, and Isabel was more reckless than he ever could have imagined. My brother never had enjoyed riding and would not have purchased any kind of horse, nor would he have encouraged anyone else to do so.

Her doctor refused to give me more information, but a nurse in the hall whispered that Isabel would recover without difficulty.

I returned the next day, and since her parents were not there, I was able to see Isabel for a few minutes. We spoke a little of Jeffrey, but I could see that she did not want my company, and there was no point in prolonging what had become an embarrassing circumstance. I went away. Later I walked by the lake and tasted ice in the air. The waves looked oddly slick, almost brittle, like glass. November has arrived without my noticing it, and here it is, black and gray and white, as hostile as a curse.

An old man passed and, without encouragement from me, said, "The worst things never happen, sir." I stopped to stare, but he shook his head and hurried off. He is wrong. The worst things do happen. For years, the worst things have been happening.

I went back to the railway station, alone this time, and boarded another train. I was lucky enough to have a small compartment for this leg of the journey, and I watched the dying landscape pass my window, with A Tale of Two Cities *open in my lap. This, indeed, is "the winter of despair." I am hungry for familiar streets and vistas. Soon!*

Once again, Kate did not read the next entry. She pressed the journal between her hands for a moment.

"Familiar streets and vistas?" Where was he from? Obviously he loved the place and was sorry to have left it. Did she feel that way about San Francisco? No. What was familiar about it had been destroyed in the earthquake. The city that was growing up now was strange to her. And she had always wanted her mother's Ireland—until she had it.

She was tempted to read the last page of the journal, but there was something exciting about reading through it one entry at a time, and then wondering about the author. He had lost it in December, so obviously he had not reached home as soon as he had hoped. What had happened to him in the meantime?

This was almost like one of the serial stories that ran in the newspapers. Wouldn't Jolie have loved it? She had been so romantic. She had been rather like Ellen, although Ellen professed to dislike everything about Jolie, whom she had only known slightly.

Poor Ellen—drat that outrageous Aaron, who had broken her heart so carelessly. Well, all Ellen needed was the responsibility of her own business, and she would have that soon enough.

Kate put the journal back in her dresser drawer and closed it with a click. Good night, she thought. Wherever you are. I hope you made it home at last.

But—who is Isabel?

Chapter 6

ELLEN

The tide was coming in, wave lapping after glittering wave, creeping over the rocks and sand, turning them dark, covering the line of dried brown seaweed left by the last high tide. The sunlight reflected from the water was blinding. Ellen tilted her broad-brimmed straw hat lower over her eyes as she watched one of the small coastal ships moving steadily north past the cove. It did not look much larger than a matchbox on the horizon.

"Who do you suppose is aboard that ship, Thalia?" she asked the girl on the grassy hillside beside her. In the first weeks of March, Ellen had found herself increasingly curious about the passengers on ships and trains, not quite willing to wish she were leaving San Francisco, but no longer content to be there. Everything was wrong, and nothing was right. She was not an adventurer, but it was taking so long to find a suitable shop to rent that she was losing the hope of independence. She felt trapped by her job and thoroughly sick of her tiresome life.

And sick of saving money. Why did everything cost so much? A new pair of much-needed shoes had cost nearly a dollar, even with her store discount.

And where was Aaron today? Was he thinking about her? Not likely.

Oh, she would like to run away! Fly like the gulls riding the air currents overhead, and come down in Paris or Rome or Madrid. But travel did not mean wings—it meant trains and boats, crowds and discomfort. She had nothing in common with Kate's friends, the Prescotts, who seemed willing to put up with anything, just so they were not in one place for very long. They would be leaving again in a few weeks, Kate had said.

Ellen had begun to think that her entire life would be lived exactly the way it was now—even if the shop were successful. San Francisco forever. Perhaps even the shabby boardinghouse forever. Sunday picnics with her brother and their friends forever. Oh, it was all so ordinary, ordinary, ordinary! Why couldn't Ma understand this and see how she longed for a different life—an exciting life?

"I think that the people on that ship are very lucky," Thalia said. "They're all rich, I guess." She sat up straight and squinted against the bright light, watching the ship.

"Would you like to be rich?"

Thalia hesitated, frowning. Then she said, "I'd like my

family to be rich. Wouldn't you? If you're rich, you can have a wonderful home, forever. You wouldn't have to worry so much." Her voice took on a bitter edge at her last words, and she looked down and began nervously pleating her dark blue cotton skirt.

Ellen did not answer. Thalia's parents had been gone for nearly four months, contributing nothing more to the girl's life than three cheap postcards and a wrinkled five-dollar bill in a soiled envelope with no return address. When were they coming back for her? Ma had written several letters to the hotel they had said they would be staying in, but the letters had been sent back, unopened. The Rutledges, mother, father, and very spoiled little son, had managed to disappear into the small and slightly disreputable world of moving-picture making. Some in the boardinghouse thought that they now might have gone to New York, where most moving-picture companies were located. They had been so convinced that their son could be a star! Poor little Oliver, who was called "Rolf" now. *Thalia* and *Rolf*, instead of Polly and Oliver. Ellen found herself smiling, more in pity than amusement. Thalia had confessed to her that her mother had changed their names with the hope that they might seem more attractive to the people who wanted child actors. But no one had been interested in the girl, no matter what she was called. Thin and gawky at twelve, she was too old for some roles—and too young for others. Only her wonderful, curly blond hair attracted attention, but it was usually uncombed and often not especially clean.

Ellen pulled off her hat and raised her face to the sun, eyes closed. Who cared if she got sunburn? Miss Franchone might rage all she wished tomorrow. Before long, Kate would find a suitable place for a shop, and then Ellen would be leaving Schuster's forever.

Even thinking the name "Schuster" caused her distress. Aaron was back from Hawaii, and she had seen him exactly twice, for hasty teas in little side-street shops where she would never run into one of her friends. There was no hope of showing him off. And he never took her anywhere else. His telephone calls were few and hasty, and his notes scribbled carelessly, not always grammatical—but always unenlightening. She wondered where people like Aaron—and the awful Rutledges—learned to be so indifferent to the feelings of others.

"I wish we could stay here forever," Thalia said, sighing deeply.

"Wouldn't that be wonderful? Hugh would like to live here, but it's too far from San Francisco to go back and forth to his job."

"People ride the ferry across to Marin County every day," Thalia said.

"That's expensive. Let's just enjoy it while we can. We'll have to go back to the cabin soon for the lunch they're fixing for us. Hugh and the McCarthys are very proud of their cooking. Even Joe is helping."

"I'll bet Mary is doing all the cooking. Men always leave things like that to women. And girls." Thalia held her bouquet of wilting wildflowers to her pale face.

Ellen stifled laughter. It was not taking Thalia long to learn the rules of the world. "Come on, let's go back and give poor Mary McFee a hand."

"Poor boy-crazy Mary," Thalia said. She looked sideways up at Ellen, and Ellen knew she was hoping for approval and acceptance. Obviously she had been eavesdropping on the kitchen conversations about Mary, who was naughtier than she should be.

"Well, Mary is . . ."

"Is crazy about Hugh and both of the McCarthys," Thalia said. "Don't you care, even a little bit?"

"No," Ellen said. She held out a hand to the girl and pulled her to her feet. "Hugh can take care of himself, and I don't want either one of the McCarthys. And you're too young to worry about things like that."

"Mama says you're never too young to think about boys."

And your mama did not do much for herself in that regard, Ellen thought, remembering Mr. Rutledge and his tight suit and his oily hair.

The cabin sat at the top of the hill, so weathered that it

was barely visible under the blooming rose vines that covered it. Long before they reached it, they could smell chicken frying. Hugh, tan as a hazelnut and with his shirt-sleeves rolled up, was sitting with his back to a tree, and he raised a lazy hand when he saw them growing closer.

"See?" Thalia hissed. "I told you. Mary is doing all the cooking."

Ellen suddenly was saturated with happiness. What could be better than this, a day in the country with her brothers and her friends, and all her worries left behind in San Francisco? She did not need to escape her life. She needed to pay more attention to the details of it. Ma always said that joy was to be found in the smallest things. Perhaps she was right after all. Well, she was occasionally right. Ellen did not plan on admitting this, however.

"Too bad Kate didn't come," Hugh said as Ellen reached him.

"She and her aunt are too busy arranging furniture, and she was going to have dinner with the Prescotts." Ellen sat down beside him and patted the grass next to her, indicating that she wanted Thalia to sit down, too. But Thalia disappeared around the side of the cabin, and Joe followed, carrying a baseball.

"She never hangs around when anybody mentions Kate," Hugh said quietly. "Why?"

Ellen leaned back against the tree. "She's jealous, I suppose. I was afraid she might be. We talked about Kate so much before she came back from Ireland. Kate seems so splendid—well, she is! Here she is, practically a child herself— "

"Never a child," Hugh corrected.

"All right. So young, then, to have traveled halfway around the world. And now she's all set up in a lovely apartment. And looking for a shop, which she will rent with hardly *any* help from me."

"Your own fault, Sis," Hugh reminded her mildly.

"Don't lecture me, Hugh. Please. I do it to myself. But I'm making up for that. I've put away nearly every cent I've made since January, and I've worked three nights a week stocking shelves in the store, for extra money. I'm catching up."

Hugh sighed. "I know. I'd like to punch Aaron Schuster in the mouth."

"And I'd like to slap Mary McFee silly, Hugh. What will that get us?"

Hugh grinned suddenly. "Don't take anything out on Mary. She doesn't deserve it."

Ellen did not respond, but now she was sure. Hugh really was interested in Kate's friend from the train. Playing indifferent, she said, "Are you going to the wedding with Kate next week?"

"What? Wedding?" Hugh said. "Are you talking about Edith Jones's wedding? It's all we ever hear about from Kate."

And from Adele, Ellen finished to herself. "Well, are you going? I wouldn't miss it."

"I'll probably go," Hugh said casually. "You girls will need somebody to help you on and off the cars."

"We will not!" Ellen said. "The day hasn't come when Kate and I need help getting on and off streetcars."

Hugh laughed and jumped up. "Let's go in and see if we can set the table or slice the bread. Call your shadow."

"Thalia!" Ellen called, and immediately the girl came around the corner, smiling. "Is it time to eat? I'm starved." Joe followed, rubbing his dirty face with dirtier hands.

They ducked under dragging rose vines hanging in the doorway and went inside. It was a perfect day. But she would have to talk to Thalia about eavesdropping. Apparently her mother did not bother with instructing her in good behavior.

When they reached home that evening, Kate was there, waiting in the kitchen with Ma. She jumped up when Ellen came in and said, "I found it!"

"Kate! What are you doing here?" Ellen asked.

"I couldn't go home after I had dinner with the Prescotts. Everything is too exciting, and I had to tell you as soon as I could. Here, sit down, Hugh. You listen to this, too. Everybody, sit down."

Ma and Mary Clare got up instead, to bring more coffee from the stove and slice more servings of the applesauce cake. Kate, flushed with excitement, leaned forward on her elbows.

"Just listen to this," she said. "The Prescotts invited a friend of my father—he was a reporter at *The Call,* too. I was telling the Prescotts how hard it is to find a small shop that is affordable and still in a part of town where we can get the customers we want, and Mr. Davidson said he knew of one—and we went to see it! It's only three blocks from the apartment, and it really is quite small, but we can afford it. And it's vacant right now. There was a hat store there, but it's gone out of business."

Hugh shook his head doubtfully. "What building? I thought I'd covered everything in that neighborhood, looking for something for you."

"It's the one with the little restaurant at one end and a bookstore at the other. And there's a tobacco shop, too, and . . ."

"I know the one you mean." Hugh took the cake his mother offered. "Lots of small hole-in-the-wall shops, and most of the people have been there forever. There are a few flats upstairs. It's old, and half of the second floor is vacant, but that's because it's all one big flat, and the owner isn't here."

"Hugh, where do you learn all these things?" Ma asked, interrupting the conversation. "Aren't you smart!"

"I looked for a flat for Kate and her aunt in the building, but I was told that the vacant one wasn't available. I didn't think about the shops—they seemed occupied."

"The hat shop just closed a few days ago," Kate said. "Mr. Davidson and I had a good look through the window. It's really tiny, but it would be perfect for us to start out in, Ellen. I wish you had come home sooner! We could have gone to see it tonight. Can you take off tomorrow morning?"

"Only if I want to be fired," Ellen said. "Frankie is dying to sack me. Can't we see it during my lunch break?"

"Yes, of course," Kate said. "But I'm scared to death that somebody will snatch it right out from under us."

"Who's handling it?" Hugh asked. "Not that reporter."

"No, but he's old friends with the man who owns the building, who is coming back to San Francisco tomorrow. Mr. Davidson's going to write an article about him—I guess he's somebody important—so he went around to look at the building again and saw the empty shop. He only noticed it because the owner's father used to run a little stationery store there a long time ago. You know, unusual writing papers and fancy pens and such. Mr. Davidson used to buy a special kind of ink there."

"So?" Ellen made a helpless gesture. "Is he going to introduce you to the owner, or what?"

"He said he would get in touch with him tomorrow. Isn't this exciting?"

"It will be, if the price is right," Ellen said. "Kate, it could be too expensive."

"Especially on that street," Hugh added gloomily.

"But it's so tiny!" Kate protested.

"I'll pray on it tonight," Ma said. "You girls need a little help. Now. Does anyone want more cake?"

"Not I. If I eat more, I'll burst," Kate said. "I'd better go home. I told Aunt I'd be late, but I didn't plan on being this late."

"I'll see you home, Kate," Hugh said, getting to his feet.

"You will not," Kate said.

"He will!" Ma said. "This is no time of night for young girls to be running around town."

"Give up, Kate," Ellen said. Then she looked around and said, "What happened to Thalia? She was right behind me."

"She ran off when she saw Kate," Mary Clare said. "Like she always does."

"She's a sneaky girl," Ma said, scowling. "I can't forgive her or forget what she did."

Ellen sighed. "Ma, she's said she was sorry. It was stupid and mean, but she's been good as gold since. She does her homework and helps around here. What more do you want?"

"Rent," Ma said. "And that's a fact."

"I'll pray on it," Ellen said, and Hugh laughed disrespectfully.

Ellen watched him leave with Kate and she thought,

Oh, I love him so much. Why can't it be Kate? Not Mary and not Adele. Why can't it just be Kate for my Hugh?

The next day began badly, as the days at Schuster's often did. Miss Franchone was furious about Ellen's sunburn and insisted on dabbing at her face with a powder puff until Ellen slapped her hand away, crying, "Stop it! That hurts!"

By lunchtime, she had shown three dresses to wealthy young women who seemed determined to be critical and left without buying anything. Miss Franchone blamed Ellen, of course. Ellen's sunburn hurt, her feet were blistered from tight shoes, and one of the other models told her that Aaron's grandmother had been in the store, selecting new table linens for a dinner party. Ellen imagined, probably correctly, that she would not be invited to that party, either.

She met Kate outside Schuster's at noon and rushed off with her to see the shop. Kate had been right—it *was* tiny, with one charming bay window overlooking the street and a pretty blue door next to it with a glass panel still bearing the painted words *Dulce Milliner.*

The two peered into the bay window, cupping their hands around their eyes in order to see better. "See the glass-topped counter?" Kate asked. "See all the little shelves? There are so many! See the drawers?"

"I see, Kate, but there hardly will be enough room for both of us behind the counter at the same time."

"I know, I know, but isn't it sweet? I think there's a storeroom in the back, but I can't see that far into the shop. Oh, look! I see a cash register. Ellen, it only needs new paint on the walls and a pretty window display, and we'll be ready to open."

Ellen laughed. "Oh, Katie, you know that it takes a lot more than that to be ready to open. Listen to your aunt. She knows all kinds of things about the retail trade."

"Retail trade," Kate said, stepping back from the shop and studying it. "Just think of us being in the 'retail trade.' "

Ellen hugged herself. "All of a sudden I'm scared to death, Kate."

"So am I," Kate said. "But I love the feeling. Oh, I hope this works out!"

"We are practically businesswomen, Kate." Ellen laughed. "I'll remember this moment for the rest of my life."

"Hey, down there!" a voice called from the second floor. They looked up to see a middle-aged man leaning out of an open window. "Kate Keely, is that you? Come upstairs immediately and let me introduce you to Mr. Woodmark." His head vanished, and a window banged down.

"That's Mr. Davidson," Kate said. She and Ellen hurried to the doors opening to the stairs that led up to the second floor. Ellen noticed that the name "Woodmark" had been carved in the stone over the door, and she pictured in her mind a man the same age as Kate's friend, perhaps a little bald, and probably rather stout.

But at the head of the stairs only one balding, stout man awaited them, and Kate quickly introduced him. The other man was much too young to be the owner of anything. He was thin and slightly stooped, and his frank blue eyes studied her critically from behind round, steel-rimmed glasses. He had a dark, neatly trimmed beard that did nothing to make him look older or more impressive. He reminded her of Aaron's college friends or some of the younger college professors.

"This is Mr. Woodmark," Mr. Davidson said, clapping the younger man on the shoulder. "His father and I were at university together, and Woodmark runs the family businesses now."

Woodmark? Ellen thought, on the verge of giggling. *This* is the great man? She held out her hand, and Mr. Woodmark shook it briefly before turning to Kate and shaking her offered hand.

"Who is the one who wants to rent the shop?" Mr. Woodmark bluntly.

"I am," Kate said.

Mr. Woodmark stared. "How old are you?"

Ellen's humor disappeared. How rude! Who did he think he was?

"I'm nearly eighteen—" Kate began.

"Nearly?" Mr. Woodmark repeated. "You aren't old enough to transact business. Don't you have a guardian?"

"My aunt—" Kate began again, only to be interrupted once more.

"You want a shop to play some sort of schoolgirl game?" Mr. Woodmark asked.

"Of course not!" Kate said sharply. "We are serious businesswomen." She went on to explain what she and Ellen would be selling in their shop. She stressed how much they knew about linens, and how much help her experienced aunt would be in setting up the business.

Mr. Woodmark watched her talk. His expression was impossible to read. Finally, when Kate ran out of words and stood before him helplessly, he said, "Interesting. Please send your aunt around, and I'll see what she has to say about all of this."

"Well!" Ellen began, but Kate nudged her painfully and said, "I'll ask my aunt to call on you this afternoon. Will that be all right?"

Mr. Woodmark studied her face and then nodded sharply. Ellen saw the scar then, for the first time. It was a thin, new-looking scar that cut down through his left eyebrow. She looked away before he caught her staring.

Some woman probably hit him with something, she thought. What an insufferable puppy! How old is *he*? Seventeen and a half?

He fixed his blue eyes on her and said, "I am twenty-six, madam, with a college degree and an inborn ability to read minds, inherited from my mother."

He turned back to Kate then and said, "I would be grateful if your aunt could come and see the shop at two-thirty. I'll be back by then, and I'll be happy to show it to her. You may come along, if you wish."

His blue eyes glanced off Ellen then and dismissed her without comment. With a short "Good-bye," he turned and walked into the open door of a flat. Beyond, Ellen saw sheet-draped furniture and not much else.

"Well, well," Mr. Davidson said, mysteriously pleased. "Woodmark doesn't like business discussions, and I was afraid that he might cut you short."

"Cut us short!" Ellen cried, exasperated. "Surely you didn't think that what we had was a polite conversation?"

Mr. Davidson looked bewildered. "He's the most charming young man I've ever known," he said. "But he doesn't like business."

"What *does* he like?" Ellen said, disgusted. "Croquet?"

"Books," Mr. Davidson said. He looked around the hall, as if expecting to find enlightenment somewhere. "Books," he repeated. "And magazines."

"Good," Kate said. "My aunt and I love books and magazines. We'll be here at two-thirty."

Mr. Davidson told them good-bye and went back into the apartment, shutting the door behind him. Ellen and Kate walked downstairs silently.

"He won't rent it to you," Ellen said as they made their way down the sidewalk. "What an arrogant man."

"We don't like business details too much either, Ellen," Kate reminded her. "Let Aunt take care of everything. If Mr. Woodmark thinks I can't manage without a guardian, let him. What we want is the shop. Stop, Ellen. Look back at it! It's perfect!"

Ellen had to admit that it was.

"We don't even know what he wants for rent," Ellen said, worrying already.

"We'll find out this afternoon, and then I'll run by Schuster's and tell you."

Ellen held up her crossed fingers. "Oh, I hope this turns out all right. I'd never be satisfied with anything else now. If only the place came without Mr. Woodmark."

"He won't come in and bother us," Kate said, sounding full of confidence. Then she grinned. "We'll hang nothing but dozens of lace-trimmed *bloomers* in the window, to make sure of it."

But Ellen, thinking of the despicable Mr. Woodmark living above the shop and perhaps criticizing everything they ever did, shook her head. If he was twenty-six, she was Thalia's age! Puppy! If he had only half of Aaron's charm, she would be satisfied.

How could Kate like him? There was no accounting for her sometimes.

Chapter 7

KATE

Kate and Aunt Grace found Ellen sitting on the top step outside their door, fanning herself with her pocketbook, when they returned to their flat shortly before six o'clock. She jumped to her feet when she saw them.

"Tell me everything that happened!" she demanded as Kate unlocked the door. "Do we have the shop?"

"We have it!" Kate said, laughing. She was carrying groceries in a string bag, and she went straight to the kitchen to put it on the table, with Ellen following her closely. "Sit down, Ellen. I'll push open the window. Heavens, it's hot in here! You look as if you were ready to faint."

"I *will* faint if you don't tell me everything," said Ellen, but she sat down at the kitchen table and peeled off her gloves. "Oh, this sunburn is simply awful! I'm on fire, and I'm sure I'm breaking out in a million freckles. I've been sitting on your steps like a beggar for half an hour, and I'd like to tear off my collar and rip it to shreds. And I would have, if your impossible old landlord hadn't been creeping up and down, watching me as if he expected me to break into your flat and steal your silver."

Aunt Grace filled a glass with water and gave it to Ellen. "Unhook your collar and give yourself a chance to breathe. And do take off your hat and let down your hair. There's no one here but us. While we're telling you all the news, we'll put dinner on the table. It's just delicatessen food, but you'll eat with us? Good."

Ellen drank half the glass of water in long gulps. "Oh, thank you. Why does water taste so good sometimes? All right, now tell me everything. Was that Watermark person insufferable to you, Miss Keely?"

"*Woodmark*. And he wasn't insufferable, not at all. I thought he was charming." Aunt Grace exchanged an amused smile with Kate over the bread she was slicing.

"He was much nicer this time, Ellen," Kate said, busy with cold roast beef. "But he talked to Aunt, mostly." She laughed a little and shook her head. "He still thinks I'm too young to know anything, but I wasn't about to argue with him. I wanted the shop too much."

"And?" Ellen asked impatiently. "And? *And?* Can we afford it?"

"Yes!" Kate said. "We've agreed—or rather, Aunt and Mr. Woodmark agreed—that we would rent the shop for a trial six months. And then he showed us around his flat."

"*His* flat?" Ellen asked. "Oh, I don't care about that. So when can we start painting the shop?"

"Tomorrow," Kate said, setting the table with the new china she and Aunt had chosen when they were furnishing their new home. "Or even tonight, if you are so anxious to begin. But listen, Ellen, let me tell you about his place. It's gorgeous. Full of antiques—"

"They're from his parents' Van Ness house," Aunt Grace said as she put butter and mustard on the table. "I remember hearing about the Woodmarks, how they died only weeks apart—that was before the earthquake—and their sons sold the big house, and the elder boy went away and the younger one began working on the magazine that his father founded. Now what was it called? Oh yes. *High Tide*. Poems and stories and interesting articles about California history. Your father never missed an issue, Kate."

"You should have told Mr. Woodmark that you remembered his family, Aunt. Especially that you remembered the magazine." Kate filled a bowl with canned tomatoes and set it on the table. "Here we go. It's not much, Ellen, but it will do until you get home to the boardinghouse for a proper meal."

Aunt Grace sat down and shook out her napkin. "I wouldn't have dreamed of talking about his family during a business meeting. He would have thought us quite unprepared for the retail world. I imagine he'll look in on us from time to time—at least, that was what he implied—"

"You mean he is going to check up on us?" Ellen asked, indignant.

Kate laughed. "What do we care? And stop picking on him, Ellen. Aunt and I rather liked him."

"I *did* like him," Aunt said as she helped herself to a thick slice of cold beef. "Oh, Ellen, you should have seen his flat. He was just unrolling one of the big carpets when we got there. Silk! And books everywhere in wonderful glass cases. And, as it turns out, he owns the bookstore on the block, too, but someone else runs it for him."

"So what does he do, then?" Ellen asked. Kate could tell from her expression that she was not about to surrender her dislike of Mr. Woodmark. But then she looked up, suddenly interested. "Or is he one of the Burlingame crowd?"

"I should think not!" Aunt said. "He didn't strike me as one of that noisy, lazy flock of conceited parrots."

Kate kept her head down to hide her expression. Aunt agreed completely with Mrs. Flannery about the general worthlessness of the crowd Ellen was so desperate to join. When she looked up again, Ellen was blushing under her sunburn.

"We didn't ask him what he did," Kate said. "He just got back to San Francisco, so I suppose he's been away on business." Kate looked up then and laughed. "I can't imagine him traveling for pleasure. He is a bit dour, if you compare him to Peter Prescott, who seems to enjoy every minute of life."

"I think Mr. Woodmark has not enjoyed a single minute of his own life," Ellen said. "But it doesn't matter. As long as we have the shop, I don't care. And why are we talking about all of this? Tell me everything about the shop!"

"It's perfect in every way," Kate said. "The storeroom is as big as the shop, which is good, because we need it. And there's a little desk back there for Aunt Grace, when she comes in to keep our books. There's even a hot plate for our coffee. And a small closet we can turn into a dressing room, if anyone wants to try on a shirtwaist—or one of the dresses that we're going to make! There's even a lavatory."

Ellen, buttering bread, said, "Now we have to decide what we're going to call the shop. I mean *really* decide. I'd still like to find a way to use our names."

"Ellen and Kate's Shop," Kate said. "Kate and Ellen's Shop." They had had this conversation many times in the boardinghouse kitchen, late at night.

"The Bloomer Shop," Ellen said, nearly choking on a bite of bread. "We'd draw crowds."

"Unmentionables Unlimited," Kate said. "We'd draw bigger crowds."

"Girls!" Aunt Grace said.

At that moment, someone knocked on the door, and Kate hurried to open it. The landlord stood there holding a paper parcel, and he thrust it at her. "Here," he said impatiently. "Some old man brought this around for you this afternoon, and when you didn't answer, he left it with me." He fished a card out of his pocket and squinted. "Somebody Logan." He handed her the card, too, and shuffled away, sighing loudly as if delivering the package had cost him ten years of his life.

Kate, both hands full, bumped the door closed with her shoulder. "It's from Dr. Logan. What can it be?"

She unwrapped it in the living room, with Ellen and Aunt Grace watching. "For heaven's sake," Kate muttered when the paper dropped away. "I don't believe it."

She held up a framed watercolor of a water lily. "Jolie painted it, and she sent it to her father. I wonder why he's given it to me." She put the painting down and turned the card over to read the message on the back. "'I'm closing the house. I thought you would like this to remember Jolie.'" Tears filled her eyes. "I wish I had been here! I'll go by tomorrow and see him."

Ellen picked up the painting, shaking her head in wonderment. "It's beautiful. Somehow I never thought of Jolie Logan being able to do something like this."

"She painted dozens of pictures," Kate said. "And she wrote short pieces about what she painted. I don't think there was anything about the water lily, though, at least not that I remember. Look at the color. It's the same blue as the shop door."

"'The Water Lily,'" Aunt Grace said slowly. "You could

call the shop that. It sounds elegant. And there's no mention of bloomers."

"I like it," Kate said. "What about you, Ellen?"

After a moment, Ellen nodded. "Yes, I like it, too. And in a way, Jolie had something to do with all of this. If she hadn't taken you to Ireland, Kate, you never would have found the factory, and we wouldn't have all those beautiful linens, and there wouldn't be a *bloomer shop*!" The last words were said with a laugh.

Kate laughed, too, and finally Aunt joined in reluctantly.

"That's it, then," Kate said. "It will be 'The Water Lily,' and we'll put the painting in the window."

"On a chest of drawers," Ellen said. "With little bits of linens peeking out of the different drawers. Just hints of what's inside. And the McCarthy boys know a sign maker."

"And I know a printer," Aunt Grace said. "We'll have cards made up."

"Let's all go over to the boardinghouse and tell everybody!" Ellen said. "This is too good to keep."

They cleared the table, put on their hats, and hurried away to the streetcar. As they boarded, they never noticed the young, bearded man standing across the street, watching them, smiling wryly, and slowly shaking his head.

The evening at the boardinghouse turned into a celebration, with the boarders joining in enthusiastically, sharing coffee and cookies in the dining room. Even Thalia, brooding and pale, wearing one of Ellen's dresses cut down to fit her, sat in a corner of the room and watched. Kate, still having to struggle to forgive the girl, smiled at her, but Thalia ducked her head and did not respond. Kate decided to waste no more time on her. The linens were stored safely in their flat, the wicker baskets stacked in both bedrooms, and there was no reason to fear any more of Thalia's tantrums.

Hugh volunteered himself, Joe, and both of the McCarthys to paint the shop, and Mrs. Flannery promised a proper party to honor the opening of The Water Lily.

But Mrs. Stackhouse, wearing the three-cornered smile that always signaled the coming of a malicious remark, said, "I don't know what times are coming to when Irish *girls* set themselves up to be shopkeepers, like men. It seems to me that certain somebodies are getting too far above themselves."

Kate, who had always despised Mrs. Stackhouse, was tired and flustered, and before she could stop herself, she snapped, "We don't all have family members paying our living expenses, like you. And we're counting on selling lots of linen goods to Irish *girls*, who know a wonderful thing when they see it."

There was a small silence, and then Matt McCarthy bellowed laughter, picked Kate up and swung her around until she protested, and kissed her. "If Ellen won't marry me, maybe you will, Katie. I could love a woman of property, especially if she's full of sass! And Irish, too!"

Everyone laughed, then, and the difficult moment passed. Both Mrs. Stackhouse and Thalia went upstairs, separately, without looking back, their mouths drawn down, their eyes averted. Kate was reminded of one of her father's fairy tales. Those two, she thought—they're like two witches leaving the christening after putting a curse on the child. She shivered and hugged herself. Our Water Lily, our child, will be safe from the likes of them!

But then, as she smoothed down her dress, which had been rumpled by Matt's enthusiastic outburst, she thought that she had never been so glad to be independent as she was that moment. Who cared what Mrs. Stackhouse and bratty Thalia thought about anything!

I *am* a woman of property, she thought. And years from now I'll remember this night as the beginning of the best part of my life. It was wonderful to be young and healthy, with everything ahead of her.

She was still excited when she and Aunt reached home late that evening, too excited to sleep. For a long time she sat by her open bedroom window, looking out over the city lights. The air was cool now, and a light wind blew. She could smell salt water instead of the dust from rebuilding that hung over the city.

I was right to come back, wasn't I? she thought. I could have refused and stayed in Ireland. But what would have happened to me then? What would have happened to Aunt Grace? No, this was the right choice. Everything will be fine.

She changed into her nightgown, washed her face, brushed her hair, and took out the travel journal.

Once she had looked ahead to see how many pages had been used. There were not as many as she had hoped. Even if she only read one or two pages a week, she would be finished much too soon—and she would never know if the man had reached his home. Or who he was. She had spent the entire trip either in the compartment or in Peter's seat, and she had become familiar only with the travelers in her own car, and Adele and Edith. When had this man become an unknown participant in her journey westward? She and the Prescotts had changed trains too many times for her even to guess. Perhaps the journal would tell her.

She turned to a new entry. What do you have to tell me tonight? she wondered. Will I get a hint of your name or where you came from?

Frederick had persuaded me to take an extra day in Omaha so that I could visit Stephen, who is to be married around Christmas, so I telegraphed him to warn him that I was coming. He met me, along with two of his friends, and they carried me and my baggage off with a great deal of racket and high spirits. We had a fine dinner, the four of us, before Stephen brought me back to his house for the night. He and I sat up late, recalling university days, and of course, we spoke of Isabel. Am I growing so old that those times seem like the best times of my life?

Kate sat very still. Isabel again.

I'm jealous, she realized. I've read only a few pages written by someone I'll never know, and I'm jealous because he underlined her name.

She was tempted to continue reading, and she nearly turned the page to the next entry. But she did not want to say good-bye to the writer any sooner than she must. With patience, she could still hope that her questions might be answered, that she might discover the name of the place he called home. And even the identity of Isabel.

He had underlined her name. Did he love her?

Had he wondered if someone had found and read his journal?

Kate put it back in her drawer and got into bed.

Who is Isabel?

Good grief, she thought. I'm as bad as Ellen. She with her Aaron, I with my stranger.

She fell asleep.

At ten o'clock the next morning, she went to see Dr. Logan. Mrs. Conner was surprised to see her at the door, but she let Kate in, warning her that Dr. Logan was getting ready to leave for the Marin County house at any moment.

"You just caught him, Kate," the woman said. "I don't know if he'll want to make time for coffee. He's set on taking the next ferry."

"I only wanted to speak to him for a moment," Kate said as Mrs. Conner closed the familiar front door behind her. "He came by our flat yesterday, but we were out."

"He told me he was giving the painting to you, and I was so glad," Mrs. Conner said. "Wait in the library, and I'll run up and tell him you're here."

Kate sat on a chair in the library for what would be the last time. Most of the furniture was gone. The bookshelves were empty. Even the window curtains had been taken down. Jolie would have hated this. She had wanted the house preserved forever exactly as her mother had kept it. But it was no place for a lonely old man.

Dr. Logan came in then, making an effort to smile. "Did you get the painting?"

Kate got up. "I can't thank you enough for giving it to me. We're naming our shop The Water Lily and putting the painting in the window. Everything is being planned around it. I thought you'd like to know that."

He blinked several times. "Jolie would have been pleased. I've heard all about your shop, from Mr. Burleigh. He's very impressed with your plans. I wish you all the good luck in the world."

"I think about Jolie so often," Kate said. "She was happy, you know. She truly was happy."

He looked down and shook his head. "Thank you for telling me that again. I try to believe you."

Kate stayed only a few minutes, and when she left, she looked back once. It was a beautiful house, almost untouched by the earthquake, representing the old San Francisco that was being crowded by the new city that was leaping up in its place. But the house was haunted now by two women, Jolie and her mother, forever moving in and out of the quiet, polished rooms, ghosts of a life that was gone.

Kate turned toward the new city and her new life.

Chapter 8

ELLEN

Ellen believed that there was no man in San Francisco who was better looking than Aaron Schuster, with his pale blond hair, dark eyebrows, and long lashes. His clothes were perfect, not too new but obviously expensive and always exactly right. The leather gloves he pulled off and stuffed in a pocket were just shabby enough to look smart.

Ellen, sitting across from him in the small tea shop, could not stop smiling, although it was not wise to let him know how thrilled she was to see him for the third time in two weeks. Did this attention mean something? Before their hurried luncheon was over, would he ask her to go out to dinner with him? Or to meet his grandmother? While her mother might scoff at the idea, Ellen had convinced herself that such a meeting would be the same as a public announcement that she was now a part of Aaron's world. In her restless nights, she could not stop thinking about that world, so vividly described in newspaper gossip columns, where his name often appeared because he was a guest at this or that party or dance. But now, suddenly, she wondered why he had never mentioned these occasions to her, or anything about the girls he knew. He was not at all like Hugh and the McCarthy boys, who did not hold back any details of their nights out, even though Ellen sometimes scolded them and demanded to know why they had not included her. Was that why Aaron never mentioned his social life? He was afraid that she might want to be included? She swallowed hard, appalled at this new and fearful understanding. But she was wrong, of course. She had to be wrong. She forced herself to smile again.

Aaron, busy with the small menu and the polite waitress, did not see her change of expressions. "We'll both have black tea, and my friend always wants brown toast, sliced thin, and marmalade, and I'll have a buttered muffin, and then bring us gingerbread squares." The waitress left and Aaron turned his gaze toward Ellen. "There. Are you going to reward me for remembering everything we ate the last time we were here? That must have been—let me see—"

"November," Ellen supplied, and immediately she regretted admitting that she had a better memory for the details of their relationship than he did. Instantly, she vowed to pretend to be somewhat absentminded. Let him be the one to claim the friendship.

"I wish you'd take more time for lunch," Aaron complained. "You don't eat enough to keep a canary alive."

"But I have to go back to work," Ellen said. "I've told you that I'm not in Miss Franchone's good graces right now." She did not explain that her weight was still the subject of unpleasant discussions in the dressing room. "She suspects that I won't be there much longer," Ellen added.

"Ah," Aaron said as the tea arrived. He thanked the waitress and then turned his attention back to Ellen. "Does she know you are going into business for yourself?" he asked, and then, suddenly, he laughed. "I can't get over it. My sister would no more launch herself on a career—and in her own shop!—than she would ask our father for a job in the store."

He had said the wrong thing, and Ellen scrambled through her mind to find a suitable excuse for his appalling lack of understanding and sympathy. If Hugh or the McCarthys had said such a thing, she probably would have responded angrily that the shop was not a trivial amusement but a way of supporting herself. Now the best she could manage was a lifted eyebrow and a delicate little shake of her head.

Their light lunch arrived, and Aaron was distracted from his amusement at the idea of a shop. Ellen swiftly changed the subject. "I like this place better than where we had lunch Tuesday."

"It's closer to the store, so you don't have to gobble and run," Aaron said. He smiled at her. "Come on, stay out with me this afternoon. We'll have a nice walk and perhaps you can show me this fabulous shop of yours. And meanwhile you can tell me the rest of your story about that wedding you and Kate went to last weekend."

Ellen thought, dismally, that she would have accepted his invitation—and endangered the job she still needed for a short while longer—if he had invited her to meet his grandmother that afternoon. She had less interest in meeting his parents, because his grandmother was the one who had the most impact on San Francisco society. And meeting his parents might indicate to others that she was willing to consider marrying him, if he asked, and she was *not* willing to go that far, not for a long time. She was not interested in meeting his younger sister, whose picture was in the newspapers every week, and she willingly admitted to herself that it was because she was jealous of the girl. But the grandmother? Surely Ellen could charm an old woman and thereby gain a small niche in that splendid society whose activities still seemed like fantasies to her—if only she had the opportunity. Aaron would see soon enough that she fitted in perfectly—if he was concerned at all. Probably she had been worrying about nothing.

"I'm leaving here in exactly twenty minutes," Ellen said firmly. "That's plenty of time to finish what I was telling you about Kate's friend's wedding."

"Oh, then skip the wedding details. Let's talk about *us*. How's this? I'll hang about the office until five o'clock, and then you and I will have our little walk and then an early dinner at that new place everybody's talking about—"

Ellen thought she had gone deaf for a moment, because her ears were actually ringing. Here was the chance she had wanted for so long. Immediately she pictured the opportunities that were being presented: The chance meetings with Aaron's friends, while dining in one of the city's smart new restaurants, and then a conversation on the way home that would fix a time on the weekend when they would meet again. . . . Everything would be all right!

The shop. She had nearly forgotten. She and Kate, along with Hugh, Joe, and the McCarthys, were painting the shop in the evenings—the walls and every small shelf and the inside of every drawer. But first, each surface had to be scraped and sanded, to satisfy the men. And each can of paint had to be mixed with colors that satisfied Kate and Miss Keely. It was taking forever. But surely she could miss one evening. . . .

Surely not! Hugh had made it clear to her that she had disappointed Kate enough for two lifetimes. No matter how tired she was, he had said, she must show up every evening after dinner to help. Her stockroom job at the store had been given up for the sake of the shop.

Everything was being given up for the sake of the shop.

"I can't," she said reluctantly. "I'm terribly sorry." And

then, risking more than she should, she said, "Perhaps after the shop opens, we can do something like that?"

"Oh, sure," he said casually. He was signaling the waitress then, asking for the gingerbread, consulting his watch, and, in his mind, already making other plans for himself that afternoon. She knew him so well.

The rest of their time together was unsatisfying, and when he walked her back to Schuster's, Ellen had to struggle to smile and pretend she was interested in his small talk. He left her with a wave, and she climbed the steps to the dressing room, thoroughly depressed.

Miss Franchone was waiting. "You're five minutes late," she said. "I sent Germaine in your place to show the new plaid. Miss Lacey likes her better than you, anyway. And you look terrible! Fat and as many freckles as a turkey egg! Just like one of those factory girls from South of Market."

Ellen gritted her teeth. The factory girls made much more money than she did. Somehow, Schuster's had decided that modeling gowns was such an honor that the models did not deserve a decent salary.

Not for much longer! Ellen told herself as she removed her hat and inspected her hair in one of the dressing room mirrors. We'll finish work on the shop and then get it ready and then open it. And I'll be done here forever.

Miss Franchone whisked back in and snapped, "Where's Lucy? Lucy! Never mind. Ellen, get out that pink silk with the beaded hem. Lucy, here you are! Dress

Ellen in the pink silk, and for heaven's sake, pull in her waist. She looks like a cow. The ladies are waiting for you, Ellen! Hurry up!"

Seething, Ellen stepped out of her plain, dark green dress and into the pink gown Lucy was holding. "I do *not* look like a cow. My waist is an inch smaller than it was."

"Ignore her," Lucy whispered. "You don't want to start perspiring in this dress. Here, pin up your hair in back. It's come down." She fussed around Ellen, tugging the waist and smoothing out a wrinkle.

Ellen, willing herself not to perspire—or lose her temper and shout—glided out of the dressing room and into the show room, where four women watched and waited. "Lovely," said one. Grateful, Ellen smiled at her and tilted her head in what she knew was an attractive angle.

The evenings spent in the shop were both a chore and a joy. Ellen, with her brothers and the McCarthys, hurried away from the boardinghouse every night after dinner and then dragged back home at eleven. But bit by bit the shop took on a new look. All the shabby paint had been scraped and sanded away, and the new paint—different shades of blue, accented with occasional touches of pale rose trim—set the tone for the small place. The McCarthys sanded the floors smooth and then waxed them. An artistic friend painted THE WATER LILY on the door's glass panel, and he also made a quaint blue sign to hang over the shop. Kate and her aunt fitted each shelf with pale blue paper from Chinatown. Finally, late in April, the last of the work was finished. The shop was ready to open.

It was only then that Ellen was free to spend time with Aaron. He had not forgotten her, as she had feared; instead, he had nearly drowned her in attention, with notes arriving daily in the dressing room at Schuster's and flowers delivered two or three times a week at home. They lunched together every day—and he talked about what they might do on the first Saturday night she was free.

At last Ellen could give notice at Schuster's, happily telling Frankie that she was opening her own shop and laughing when the awful woman predicted failure for The Water Lily. And on that final Friday, during lunch, Aaron told Ellen his plans. But they were not what she had wanted so much.

"Guess what?" he had asked after ordering for them. "I've got a wonderful idea for dinner tomorrow. The family of a friend of mine—he's a great pal, but he's in San Diego right now—the family has a cabin across the Bay. It's just for larking around, you know—mostly for the kids. But we've had some great parties there. Some of us decided that it would be fun to fix dinner there on Saturday and spend the evening. I've got the key and the family won't mind—they never do. What do you think?"

What friends? she longed to ask. The *right* friends?

The boys you knew in college? Girls who are friends of your family?

"What friends?" she asked.

"Oh, just friends," he said, offhandedly. "You'll like them. They're lots of fun. The girls all bring food—you don't mind, do you? And we fellas will bring ourselves."

"A sort of picnic?" she asked. Something was bothering her. His casual, sideways glance, his almost rueful laughter, hinted that he had done this before. He had taken other girls to this cabin for picnics. With friends he did not care to name.

"Exactly!" he said. "A picnic. I know you like them. You're always running off to picnics with your pals. So now you'll make some new friends. Are you game?"

Game? It was almost a challenge. A hundred warnings from her mother were sounding in the back of her mind, but Aaron was smiling at her, reaching out to take her hand.

"Say yes!" he pleaded. "Then, if you aren't sick of me, maybe I'll pick you up Sunday afternoon and we'll surprise old Gran around four in the afternoon and refuse to leave until she gives us tea. Please say yes!"

It was the "Open Sesame!" she had waited for all this time. But there was a problem, as usual. "I don't know if I should. Everyone's giving us a party Sunday evening, to celebrate The Water Lily. I'd have to be home before six."

"You'll be there!" he said. "So do we have a plan?"

"Yes," she said, and she looked down at her plate where her chicken salad lay on a lettuce leaf. She could not eat now. She was too happy. She would make sure that Grandmother Schuster liked her. Perhaps even loved her at first sight.

"Time for you to head back to work," the son of Schuster's owner said cheerfully. If he was unconscious of his snobbery, she was not, and she gritted her teeth. No one cared if Aaron returned from lunch on time or not.

But she was going to meet his grandmother on Sunday, and nothing else really mattered. So she was expected to provide food for a picnic on the day before that great event? She would do it, and so generously that Aaron would praise her.

On the way back, he asked if she would bring "sandwiches or something the guys can get their teeth into," and she agreed. She did not consider until late afternoon that preparing a lot of picnic food in the boardinghouse kitchen could not be concealed from Ma. And Ma would have questions to ask!

She stopped at a delicatessen on the way home and bought sliced ham, bread, pickles, and bakery cookies, and then concealed the package inside a Schuster's bag that she had brought with her for just that purpose. Ma would surely smell the food if Ellen tried to hide it in their bedroom, so she put it in an empty hatbox in the third-floor storeroom. After a sleepless night, she had invented the perfect excuse for getting away Saturday afternoon.

"Germaine is having a birthday party across the Bay," she told her mother in the kitchen before breakfast. "Everyone is going."

"Not that Miss Franchone, I hope," Ma said as she beat eggs in a bowl. "She sounds like the kind of woman who can spoil a wedding just by walking past the church the day before."

"No, not her," Ellen said, warming to her tale. "No one would go if Frankie had been invited."

"What about Lucy?" Mary Clare asked. She had never met the crippled woman who dressed Ellen, but she loved hearing about her. Lucy was a wonderful example of someone who did not let challenges get in her way.

"Lucy wouldn't miss it," Ellen said.

"What are you giving Germaine?" Ma asked as she tipped the eggs into a frying pan.

"Umm," Ellen said. "She said she didn't want gifts."

"Well, at least you could bring some food," Ma said. "I'll fix you up a nice package of sandwiches and cookies. How about that?"

Ellen, thinking of the ham upstairs, nodded. What else could she do now? "That would be wonderful, Ma. I'm sure she'll appreciate it."

But as she left the kitchen, Mrs. Stackhouse, lurking in the dining room, smirked knowingly at her. She—or

Thalia—always seemed to overhear everything—and guess everything else. Could she know? Impossible. Mrs. Stackhouse automatically thought the worst of everybody—and unfortunately, she always found ways of putting her thoughts into words at the most awkward times.

While Ellen climbed the stairs, she asked herself what "worst" Mrs. Stackhouse could be thinking of her. Then, grimly, she answered her own question. Obviously, the truth was the "worst." She actually had agreed to spend the late afternoon and evening with Aaron in a cabin with people whose names she did not know. Ma would have a fit, and she should not worry her mother, who had not seemed well recently. And Hugh would . . . do worse than have a fit, probably.

But this could all be innocent, as innocent as the picnics she and Hugh spent with the McCarthys and Mary McFee. No one ever challenged them. But, of course, Ellen knew them all—had known them all for years. Aaron had supplied the word "friends" too casually. Just declaring that these unknown people were "fun" was not enough. It certainly would not be enough for Ma.

Ellen sat on her bed for a long time, wondering what to do. Call Aaron and hope to reach him at home? Tell him something had come up and she could not spend the day at the cabin?

Now she was ashamed. He had not even offered to come to the boardinghouse to pick her up, but just told her to watch for him at the ferry dock on the other side of the Bay.

But the day after, Sunday . . .

He had not firmly invited her to meet his grandmother. He had only tossed out the suggestion casually, as one threw bits of food to a begging dog.

Ellen pressed the heels of her hands against her eyes. Why can't I be like Kate? she wondered. Everything is so easy for her. She doesn't want things that are impossible. Well, at least she doesn't want foolish things that are impossible.

I have to decide something!

But at that moment, a loud argument broke out downstairs. It did not involve the McCarthys, for once. Were those the Rutledges, back at last? Ellen jumped up and ran out of the room, in time to see the weeping Thalia running up the stairs to the third floor. Ellen hesitated, wondering if she should follow.

Ma's voice rose downstairs. "I did not promise you anything!" she cried. "You didn't pay the rent on the room. What did you expect me to do? I rented it out, and I've been letting your girl live here for free on the third floor, and feeding her, too."

Ellen ran down the stairs, to find her mother standing, hands on hips, in front of oily Mr. Rutledge, while Mrs. Rutledge, holding fat little Rolf, tossed her head indignantly.

"We sent money!" Mr. Rutledge protested. "If you didn't get it, you can't blame us! We sent you plenty of money. Now we expect to move into our room and have everything the way it was."

"Someone else lives there now," Ma said. But Ellen could sense that her mother was considering solutions to this problem. "Thalia's room is too small for all of you. And then there's the matter of the back rent. I didn't receive it, so as far as I'm concerned, you didn't send it. I've been through this before with boarders, and I know that getting the rent to me is your legal responsibility. So as far as I'm concerned, you'll have to pay me what you owe me before I'll even show you the only vacancy I have."

The Pickerells had left two days before, so there was an empty double room across from the McCarthys. Two cots would have to be moved in for the children—and it would be terribly crowded.

"I'll have to talk to my lawyer about that," Mr. Rutledge said, rocking back and forth on his heels. "He might not like hearing how you're trying to hold us up."

"Pay up or leave," Ma said. "And I'll thank you to take your daughter with you. You can send your lawyer around to see me any time you like."

"I'm hungry!" howled Rolf. "I want something to eat."

Ma held out her hand. "Pay up," she said.

Mr. Rutledge dug into his pocket and brought out a

roll of bills. He peeled off several and thrust them at Ma. "All right, this should settle up, but my lawyer is going to have plenty to say about this. Now give us our room."

"It's not the one you had," Ma said, pocketing the bills. "I've only got one empty room. But you can have the old one when it becomes vacant."

"I'm hungry!" Rolf wailed.

Ellen left her mother to deal with the Rutledges and fled to the kitchen. "The Rutledges are back," she told Mary Clare.

"Well, I'm sorry to hear that!" Mary Clare exclaimed. "They're such a bother and didn't we think we were done with them forever? What's going to happen to Thalia, do you suppose?"

"She's hiding up on the third floor," Ellen said. "I have a hunch that she wasn't overjoyed to see them. She looked embarrassed, and she was crying."

"Sometimes I feel sorry for her." Mary Clare, scraping the mold off a block of cheese, paused and then said, "I wonder if she wouldn't rather be in the orphanage. The sisters are good to them girls, and they don't all turn out bad afterward."

"Oh, no, that would be awful!" Ellen said. "One way or another, she'll have to stay here." The girl's precarious life caused Ellen to feel almost overwhelmed with gratitude for her own.

But then, there was this picnic, now only hours away. Oh, to be Thalia's age again, and not have to worry about meeting the right people.

The Rutledges moved into their new room, with many complaints and a flood of noisy weeping from Rolf. Thalia crept downstairs finally, to be reluctantly reunited with her flamboyant parents and chubby little brother. Ma and Mary Clare shoved two cots into the room before lunch, and peace returned to the boardinghouse at last.

Ellen retrieved the bag of food from the third floor, considered throwing it out, but then decided that it, along with the food Ma was preparing, would be a generous contribution to whatever was being provided by the other girls.

The afternoon dragged on. Ellen changed her clothes twice, finally deciding that her best choice would be the dark blue cotton and the clever little white hat with the red feather. Ma was busy with early preparations for dinner—and complaining to anyone who would listen about the Rutledges—so she did not question Ellen taking the picnic food she had prepared with no more comment than, "I'm leaving now for the birthday party, Ma."

I'll concentrate on tomorrow, she told herself.

Aaron met her, as he promised, when she stepped off the ferry. He handed her a rose and took the bags of food from her. "You brought a lot. You must have expected us to be hungry."

"You didn't tell me how many would be here, or what the other girls were bringing," Ellen said. "Who's come?"

"I don't know," Aaron said. "I haven't been out there yet. Hurry along, woman! I'm using the auto that belongs to my friend's father, so we're practically there. This is going to be great fun."

Great fun. He had used those words again.

And how could he have his friend's auto if he had not been at the cabin and did not know, yet, who was there? But she chided herself for being silly and looking for problems. What was wrong with her?

Suddenly Ellen wished she were home, helping Ma and Mary Clare in the hot kitchen. The familiar, which always seemed so boring to her, now seemed safe and even desirable.

She would remember her wish for a long and bitter time.

Chapter 9

KATE

By seven o'clock Sunday evening, nearly all of Kate's friends were there, crowded into the double parlors and the long dining room of the Flannerys' boardinghouse to celebrate the opening of The Water Lily. As soon as Mrs. Flannery and Mary Clare returned home from mass that morning, the party preparations began in the kitchen. Since the boarders were invited, most of them did not complain about the simple lunch or the dinner stew.

Well, Kate thought as she looked out over the crowded rooms, Mrs. Stackhouse and the Rutledges complained, but that was nothing new. They were invited to the party, too, in spite of their sulking and grumbling. And in spite of their unhelpful remarks. Mr. Rutledge, who professed to know everything about business, had teetered on the creaking back two legs of his chair after lunch, picking his teeth and occasionally polishing the nails of his free hand on his vest, and solemnly predicting early failure for the shop.

Mrs. Rutledge had said that nobody was wearing linen "dainties" these days except brides, and therefore, the shop had to fail. And Mrs. Stackhouse had more to say than usual about uppity Irish girls who did not know their places. "My mother always said they made good servants, if you kept after them," she had concluded, and Mrs. Flannery shot her a look that would have blistered a boot sole.

Ellen had called them all ridiculous, behind their backs, of course. But Kate had fretted about the speculations. She was not superstitious, she told herself, but hearing about failure made what lay ahead of them seem doomed. Why would those people bring it up if they did not see the future more clearly than she?

Why had she invested so much of the money in this mad plan? If the shop failed, what could she do to take care of Aunt Grace?

Now that most of the guests had assembled, Kate found herself searching faces, expecting to see her own worries reflected on them—or even worse, ridicule. But when they glanced at her, they only smiled. Even Ellen was smiling now, although earlier she had been unusually silent, brooding and sometimes tearful, and unwilling to explain. Yesterday's birthday party had unsettled her, perhaps because she was sorry that soon she would not be seeing her friends at the department store every day. But all of them were invited to tonight's party—except the dreaded Miss Franchone, of course. Ellen watched the door, probably for them. Every time the phone rang, she nearly jumped out of her clothes.

The shop was opening tomorrow, on what surely would be another hot and dusty day in the city. Kate had never been aware of the effects weather had on business, but her aunt had impressed her with the importance of it, and now she had an additional worry.

"What are you doing, standing all by yourself?" Hugh demanded. Kate turned to force a smile at him. He looked splendid in a dark suit. "Get out there and circulate," he told her. "You're a celebrity."

Kate shook her head. "No, we're two foolish Irish girls, opening their own shop on a San Francisco side street, so that they can sell underwear. I just realized how ridiculous this is."

Hugh grinned and bent his head a little so that he could make himself heard over the din. "Ellen talks about the dresses you'll be selling."

"Three dresses," Kate said. "That's all we had time to make. And we're a long way from being a dress shop. We've ordered more linen goods from the factory in Ireland, so we'll concentrate on that."

Ellen pushed through the crowd and handed her brother a glass of punch. "You look so hot." Ellen looked warm, too, and there were dark circles under her eyes.

"It's like an oven in here," Hugh said. "If we weren't so

busy at the construction site, I'd take off for some place like Half Moon Bay and not come back for a month."

"I believe you would," Kate said, but she was remembering cool Irish shores, with the clean surf curling and breaking over long reaches of sand and rocks. Hugh is like me, she thought. We may try to forget, but we still see smoking wreckage and falling dust in our dreams.

And then she saw Adele Carson coming in. "Hugh, here's Adele! Let's go say hello."

She barely noticed Ellen's quick frown as she grabbed Hugh's hand and pulled him through the crowd. Adele saw them coming, all smiles and blushes. She likes Hugh, Kate thought. Good. Hugh needs a girl to pamper him, someone who wasn't here when the city fell down around us.

Hugh did not need encouraging. Kate left him with Adele and greeted two of the women Ellen worked with at Schuster's, Germaine and Betty. "I'm glad you're here," Kate told them. "I know she saw you yesterday, but she's going to miss working with you." Betty looked startled, but Germaine hastily said, "We'll miss her, too, and we wish the two of you all the luck in the world." And then she actually dragged Betty away before the girl had a chance to say a word. But Kate was too busy to think about it for long.

The McCarthys began the toasts to the success of The Water Lily. Matt went first, and by the time he had finished, everyone in the room was laughing. Luke, not to be outdone by his elder brother, announced to the crowd that he would be glad to marry Ellen and spare her the life of a working girl, if only she would say the word.

"That word is 'no,'" Ellen said. But she stood on tiptoe to kiss Luke's cheek, and the look on his face told Kate that he might have meant what he said if he had ever had more encouragement. She flashed a glance at Hugh, to see what he thought of this, but Hugh was deep in conversation with Adele again. Kate smiled to herself.

After a while the guests began leaving, each carrying a few of the cards Aunt Grace had ordered printed. *The Water Lily,* the card said, over a drawing of the flower. Kate's and Ellen's names were in small, delicate letters in the lower left corner, over the shop's address. "Give the cards to your friends," she said over and over. "Let them know where we'll be."

Hugh kept Adele behind, telling her that he would take her home when he drove Kate and Aunt Grace back to their flat—he had borrowed an automobile. Kate expected that he would take her and Aunt home first, and he did. He let them out in front of the apartment house entrance and barely said good-bye before turning the auto away from the curb.

"Is Hugh fond of that girl?" Aunt asked as they climbed the stairs. "She's awfully sweet."

"*Almost* sweet enough for him," Kate said.

"Kate! You're not sorry, are you?"

"Certainly not!" Kate said. "But we owe so much to Hugh that I don't think there's a girl in the world who is really his equal." She unlocked the door and let Aunt go in ahead of her.

Aunt took off her hat and jacket in the hall. "Do you want a cup of tea before bed?"

Kate yawned hugely. "No. I'm ready to drop to the floor and sleep right here. At least, I hope I'll be able to sleep. Tomorrow's the day. How did it come so soon? I don't feel nearly ready."

"Everything *is* ready," Aunt said. "Everything is in place. All you have to do is unlock the door in the morning and turn the door sign over so that it reads, 'Open.'"

Kate turned to her aunt. "Tell me this will work, Aunt. I need to hear it."

Aunt Grace took both Kate's hands. "*This will work.* You'll be a great success. And you're hardly more than a child, Kate! Just look how grand you are!"

Kate considered reading a page in the journal before going to sleep, but changed her mind. She was too full of thoughts of herself to appreciate someone else's inward struggles.

~

Aunt did not go to the shop with Kate in the morning. They had decided before that there would be nothing for her to do the first day, and sitting at the little desk in the storeroom would be lonely and boring for her, so Kate went to work alone. She would not let herself think about failure on that bright morning.

Ellen was already there, wearing her dark green apron embroidered with a water lily and dusting the counter. She looked up, smiling, when Kate unlocked the door.

"Are you excited?" she asked.

"Only half mad with excitement," Kate said. She pushed back the dark green curtain that separated the stockroom from the shop, took off her coat and hat, and put on her own green apron. When she pushed back the curtain again, she saw Ellen carefully folding the dusting cloth into a small, neat square.

"I've been thinking," Ellen began as she put the cloth on its shelf under the cash register. "Some people inherit money and social connections—and never mind that their grandparents were gamblers or illiterate miners—and I've envied them every day since I was eight, when I saw a dozen girls my age going into the Palace Hotel for a birthday party. Those dresses, Kate! The pretty shoes and their curls and ribbons—I promised myself that one day I'd be a part of that world, and that shabby old house South of Market would only be a bad memory. Well, that's all it is now, a bad memory. The quake destroyed it. But I'm no closer to birthday parties in expensive hotels than I've ever been, and those little girls are all grown up and I see them in the society pages all the time." She looked so earnest that Kate was afraid she was about to cry. "But all of a sudden," Ellen continued, "on my way here this morning, I realized that this shop is more important to me than anything else has ever been. I was awake for hours last night, wishing . . . oh, it doesn't matter. I was wishing for stupid things, and I felt sorry for myself because they were out of reach. And always would be. I can see that now. But on the way here, I remembered the cards your aunt handed out last night. My name was on them. *My name*, Kate! Not one of those silly little girls going into the hotel has her name on anything but her visiting cards."

Kate was silent for a moment, and then she said, "Do you realize that that was the longest speech you've ever given? And I couldn't have been happier to hear it." She smiled and took a deep breath. "Now—let's unlock the door! We're in business."

Aunt came in, at ten-thirty, with three friends from church. Mrs. Flannery and Mary Clare rushed in, too, shortly afterward. Each lady bought a pair of linen drawers, and after they all left, Kate and Ellen had the great pleasure of restocking the shelf from the back room.

But then, for the rest of the day, only a few women came in, and they just looked around. No one bought anything. The last one was Mrs. Stackhouse, who examined the linens, which she had seen before, with an expression that meant to convey disdain and amusement.

"I suppose you girls know that Castle's having a sale on undergarments today," she said. "I was there at noon, and I swear that every Irish girl in the city was spending her lunchtime picking over the corset covers and drawers. Cotton is good enough for them, and at forty-nine cents each! Well, who wants this fancy linen, I'd like to know?"

Kate, busy folding up the things that Mrs. Stackhouse carelessly scattered over the counter, said calmly, "We'll be serving what is called 'a distinctive class.'"

"'Distinctive!'" Mrs. Stackhouse echoed. She laughed. "I'll come back when you put all this on sale. I might be interested in your bed linens then. The Flannery sheets are so rough."

She marched out, head high, and Kate watched her leave without comment. But the moment the door shut behind her, she said, "Good lord! What if that horrible old woman is right?"

Ellen shook her head. "She is *not* right, Kate! We just need to be discovered. You know as well as I do that everybody would rather have handmade things! You'll see. Mrs. Stackhouse might sneer at us, but women will come in."

Kate did her best to hide her feelings, but she was so

nervous that she was ready to cry. "What if we're wrong? We may have counted on what will never happen."

Ellen sniffed. "Why are we talking like this? We'll appeal to everybody, once the word gets around."

"I'm trying to believe you," Kate said. "Yesterday I was afraid the shop was a mistake, but on the way here this morning, I was sure it was a good idea. Now I'm not sure again."

"You're letting Mrs. Stackhouse do that to you?" Ellen exclaimed. "I'm going to ask Ma to throw her out. Once I tell her what she said to you, Ma just might do it, too!"

"Oh, Ellen! Her son pays her rent for months at a time. Your mother can't get rid of her."

"We'll see," Ellen said, but she sounded more subdued now.

In the end, Kate thought, money was always the reason decisions were made in the ways they were made. It was always money!

"I hate those little girls!" Ellen said suddenly.

"What little girls?" Kate asked, astonished at Ellen's tone of voice.

"The little girls outside the hotel when I was eight. We *will* succeed! We will amaze the whole city! The Water Lily will be famous, and so will we. Everybody will envy us, even Mrs. Stackhouse."

"If only she will admit it," Kate said.

"I'll squeeze it out of her!" Ellen declared.

~

But the day ended with only one other sale. Adele came in just before closing, to buy a set of embroidered pillowcases for her grandmother's birthday. Kate took special care folding them in tissue paper and sliding them into a blue gift box.

"Tell your friends about us," Ellen said. She sounded so cheerful, so full of confidence, that Kate was amazed. The long, silent afternoon had not bothered her.

"I will!" Adele said. "I'm taking a typing class every morning now—my grandfather's idea!—and I'll tell all the girls in class. They'll want nice things."

"That's what we're offering—nice things," Ellen said.

"So you're going to be a secretary?" Kate asked.

Adele sighed. "Grandfather thinks so. But from what I see, working in an office is no better than working in the shirtwaist factory. You're in trouble if you talk or laugh. You're fired if you're late or want to use the lavatory or get a drink of water. Or they find somebody who is willing to work for a penny less a day. Somebody's got to begin standing up for working people."

"You and Hugh—and your unions," Kate said, laughing.

When Adele left, Ellen said, "She only came in because of Hugh. But who cares? If she tells her friends in the typing class, who knows where it will lead?"

"I wish we could afford a newspaper advertisement," Kate said. "But it's so expensive."

"Let's ask your aunt to go around to the papers and ask again," Ellen said. "She knows all kinds of newspaper people, doesn't she? From when your father worked on *The Call*? Maybe someone will do her a favor. Don't worry, Kate! This is going to work out wonderfully well. I just know it."

"You've told Aaron, of course," Kate said. "I know we're competition for his father's store, but—"

"I wouldn't ask Aaron for help if I were drowning!" Ellen exclaimed. She walked away, whisking through the curtain into the storeroom.

Kate held her breath for a moment, and then she thought, Thank goodness that's over with. He's done enough to hurt her. Now he's out of her life.

Several women, friends of Mrs. Flannery's, came in on Tuesday, looking for linen collars. Kate and Ellen spread out a dozen on the counter, plain ones, collars with lace, collars with embroidery, and a few with both. The women did not hesitate, but bought them all, and when they left, Kate and Ellen had the pleasure of ransacking the storeroom looking for the box that contained the rest of them.

"What would we do without your mother and her friends?" Kate asked.

"Oh, they are coming in strictly out of pity for us," Ellen said. "I'm waiting to see what will happen with Adele and her friends in the class. If we could interest students, we might find a market among the college girls."

"Who have money to buy things," Kate said. She took a handful of collars out of the box and exclaimed, "They need ironing, and we don't have one here!"

"It's almost lunchtime. I'll take them home and iron them. Ma always has a couple of irons on the back of the kitchen stove. I'll be back before you miss me." Ellen took off her apron, put the collars in a box, and hurried away, leaving Kate alone in the shop.

It would be mad to worry that she might be overwhelmed with customers, she told herself. But how wonderful it would be. A steady trickle of people passed the shop, and many of the women stopped to look in the window. Kate liked watching them while they studied the watercolor she had propped up on a chest of drawers. Nearly everyone smiled at it. Then their gazes drifted down, where the drawers were open a few inches, allowing bits of linen and lace to hang out artfully. In front of the chest, Kate had put a scrap of blue carpet Hugh found somewhere, and she had pleated a lace-edged pillowcase there. A dozen handkerchiefs fanned out next to it, displaying lace and embroidery. Around them lay scattered pale blue paper flowers, treasures from Chinatown. Clearly the window display was a great success, but it was not bringing in customers that day.

Then a man stopped. Mr. Woodmark! Kate hoped that he would not come in, but after studying the window display for a while, he opened the door.

Kate felt herself blush. Was he checking up on them?

"Your window is quite handsome," he said. He did not look at her, but glanced around the shop instead, finally walking close to the three dresses that Ellen had hung on the wall across from the counter. "So you are selling dresses, too?"

"We only have three, so far," Kate said. "But we thought we might—"

"Who made these?" Mr. Woodmark asked.

"I made two and Ellen made one, the pink one."

He adjusted his glasses, as if to see better. "They're nice. Simple and well-made."

"Thank you," Kate said, wishing furiously that he would go away. How could she be expected to continue a conversation about sewing with a man?

"Will the two of you be making other dresses?" he asked. He was looking at the shop window now, where a linen sheet hung down the back of the chest of drawers, hiding a rather ugly unpainted wood panel.

"Yes. We like to sew."

"Surely you don't hope to compete with the big stores,"

he said. He turned to face her now, and although he was smiling, Kate still wished he would disappear.

"We sell goods that are quite different from anything being offered anywhere else. All our things are made of linen imported from Ireland."

He nodded. "I remember what you told me the day we met. I'm curious about the name of the shop, and that wonderful watercolor in the window."

So Kate told him about Jolie, the time she spent working for the girl, their trip to Ireland, and Jolie's death. Mr. Woodmark listened intently, his head bent a little, as if he were looking at something just below the level of the counter.

"And your parents are dead," he said when she finished. "You have only your aunt? They didn't die in the earthquake, did they?"

"No, before that," Kate said. She wanted to ask about his family—Aunt had said that his parents had died, too—but she was afraid to seem inquisitive. But wasn't *he* inquisitive?

Or perhaps he was only interested in knowing about her so he could better protect his property.

The door opened again, and a couple came in, a girl not much older than Kate and a blond young man. Mr. Woodmark turned to look.

"Woodmark!" the young man said. "What a surprise! I had no idea you were interested in women's—umm—unmentionables."

"Schuster," replied Mr. Woodmark coldly, as if the name alone was enough to explain their entire history and his complete opinion of the man. Then he nodded to the girl. "Excuse me, Miss Schuster. I hope you're well." He did not sound as if he hoped anything of the kind.

Kate was nearly reeling. This must be Aaron! And he had brought his sister to the shop. Why? Ellen would be . . . what? Kate did not know. A week before, she might have been devastated to have missed them. But now, after her abrupt change of mind about Aaron, she might be glad she was home ironing collars.

Miss Schuster blushed prettily and fussed with her gloves. "How have you been, Mr. Woodmark?" she asked. "We haven't seen you for a long time."

"I've been out of town," he said, without expression. He turned then to Kate and said, "Thank you for letting me see your shop. I can see that it is in good hands. Tell your aunt that I asked after her." And then he was gone.

Kate stared after him, until Aaron Schuster brought her back to reality. "Good grief, don't tell me that you're Kate? And you and Ellen are renting this quaint little place from Woodmark? He'll be a tyrant of a landlord, I can promise you."

"Aaron!" simpered his sister. She tapped his arm with gloved fingers. "Don't say that."

Her brother ignored her. "Where's Ellen? I brought my sister around to see if there's anything in the shop she might like, but we wanted Ellen to be the one to show us your goods."

Kate almost panicked. What would Ellen want? Should Kate try to delay them until Ellen returned? Or should she get rid of them? Aaron might not come back soon.

"Ellen is out right now," Kate said. "I'm not certain exactly when she'll be back."

"So you're not besieged with business, then?" Aaron asked, grinning. "Well, girls shouldn't get such high-flying ideas."

Kate, about to answer angrily, held her temper with difficulty. She directed her attention to the sister, who was flipping the skirt of the pink dress Ellen had made. "Would you like me to take that down for you?" she asked.

The girl giggled. "Of course not," she said. "I wouldn't wear something like that."

Kate would not have been surprised to have seen spots before her eyes. It had not always been easy for her to control her temper, and now, on Ellen's behalf, she wanted nothing more than to throw Miss Schuster bodily out of the shop. Instead, she said, "That's good, because the waist is much too small for you. Miss Flannery made that, and she fitted it to herself."

Aaron laughed loudly, but his sister turned red and started for the door. He followed, but he looked back over his shoulder at Kate and said, "Maybe I'll be back without my spoiled little sister."

Kate turned her back. The door closed and she was alone again.

What was she going to tell Ellen?

An elderly woman came in to look at sheets and pillowcases, and she surprised Kate by buying an entire set. Ellen returned before the woman left, and she raised her eyebrows at Kate. Kate smiled and thanked the woman.

As soon as the door closed again, she said, "Aaron Schuster was here with his sister." It was best, she had decided, to get it over with.

Ellen flushed. For a moment, she said nothing. And then she cleared her throat and said, "I can't tell you how surprised I am. But I'm glad I missed him."

Kate longed to know what had happened between them, but she knew it would be useless to ask Ellen. And it would be rude, too. Whatever it was, Ellen had changed because of it.

"Mr. Woodmark was here when they arrived," she said. "You'll be happy to know that he obviously despised Aaron."

"Both of them are insufferable," Ellen said. She had composed herself by then, and she opened the box and took out the freshly ironed collars. "Do you think we should wear linen collars? To show off our goods, I mean."

"That's a wonderful idea. Now, did you eat something when you were home?"

"Does anyone ever go through my mother's kitchen without having food shoved at her? Yes, I had a few bites, and Mary Clare helped me iron. Now you run home for lunch and tell your aunt about the collars. Before the week is over, she'll have to come in and enter our sales in her books. We're practically successful."

"I wouldn't go that far," Kate said as she took off her apron. "But who knows what might happen next?"

She went to bed exhausted that night, but she was satisfied. Perhaps they had not been really busy, but people did come in. They might tell others about The Water Lily, and more people would come to see what those brave young women were selling in their shop with the blue door.

Chapter 10
ELLEN

For the first few minutes after Kate had told Ellen that Aaron had been in the shop, she was not sure how she should react. He had brought his sister? Then he must have wanted them to become acquainted. Once she would have been delighted, but now she was angry and disgusted. How *dare* he expect such a thing, after what he had attempted? After what she had said to him?

She did not need him. Everything she had wanted was still possible, through her own efforts. She busied herself around the shop, imagining that someday she and Kate would have a bigger one, or even more than one! She would be admired. Doors would be opened to her. Her photographs would be in the newspapers, too. "The lovely Miss Ellen Flannery and her friends celebrate the opening of another Water Lily."

The truth of the matter was that Aaron's sudden surprise appearance probably meant no more than any of his whims. Her entire experience with him had consisted of silences and then rushes of superficial attention. No, she could never count on him for anything except his being insensitive and unpredictable, but now she was cured. One hideous weekend of lies and betrayal had been the medicine.

By the time the day was over, she had more control of her emotions, and she was able to smile when she said good-bye to Kate.

She made several promises to herself on the streetcar, but she broke them all within minutes of reaching home. "Did anyone telephone me?" she asked her mother as she walked into the kitchen. She had broken Promise Number One without even thinking. She had meant *never* to ask it again. Let others seek *her* out.

"Yes," Ma said. "Not ten minutes ago." She was pulling two sheets of biscuits out of the oven, her face flushed, small tendrils of damp hair clinging to her forehead. "Move the breadboard, Mary Clare, please!" She ran a spatula under each biscuit and flipped it expertly to a platter. "It was Germaine. She has such a nice voice. I asked her if she had had voice lessons, and she—"

"Ma!" cried Ellen. "For heaven's sake! What did she want?"

Ma raised her head. "What on earth? Such a racket! I didn't ask her what she wanted. She said she'd get in touch with you later this evening, or maybe tomorrow, or sometime soon."

"Not that she'll have a chance," Ellen muttered. "The boarders are always using the telephone, even though you've told them and told them that they can only make one call a day or they have to pay you more. And the Rutledges! When I passed the phone coming in here, there he was again, talking and smoking and bragging and scratching his stomach. I could . . . I could just *kill* him!"

Her mother scowled, but Mary Clare covered her mouth with both hands to stifle a laugh. "What happened to leave you in such a state, missy?" Ma demanded.

Suddenly exhausted, Ellen plopped down on a chair and leaned her elbows on the table. "I'm tired. We had customers—not many—and we sold a few things. But we haven't made enough profit so far to buy seeds for a canary. And now I'm wondering if I've lost my mind completely." Promise Number Two was broken. She was not going to complain about the shop, but that was exactly what she had done.

"It must take time for a business to build up," Ma said. She sounded doubtful. But then she added briskly, "Word of mouth will do it. We're telling everybody about the shop, and women will go there, if only out of curiosity. You'll see. By the time summer is over, you'll be holding your own. What does Kate say?"

Ellen sighed. "You know Kate. She could be worried sick, but she'd never say anything much about it. I wish I were like her. She could wash up on a beach somewhere and have a house built and a pantry full of food before the first week was out."

"Where would she get the food?" Mary Clare asked. Ellen could only gape at her. Trust Mary Clare to be interested in the finest particulars of a situation.

"Maybe it floated in on the tide," Ma said. "They say you can find anything on the beach after a high tide—even packing crates of goods from ships that went down somewhere out on the ocean. Once I read about a sick man who found a nice new coffin on the beach, and he was buried in it."

"Well, Ma, that's a cheerful thought," Ellen said as she got to her feet. "I can always count on you to put me right."

Every bone in her body ached. As she left the room, she unpinned her hat and removed her coat. Half a dozen boarders stood around the windows, gossiping while they waited for the first signs of dinner being served. Mrs. Stackhouse looked over her shoulder at Ellen, but she did not speak to her, and Ellen was grateful for that. The last thing she needed was sarcasm or ridicule. In the hall, Mr. Rutledge was on the phone again, scowling and saying, "But I told you—no, that's not what I said—no, I did not—"

The front door opened and crashed shut, and the

McCarthys thundered upstairs, laughing. Hugh came in behind them, and he seemed surprised to see her.

"You home already?" he asked.

"Where did you think I'd go?" she snapped. "Out to a restaurant to spend some of our profits?" She ran up the stairs ahead of him and slammed her bedroom door shut behind her.

Somewhere, water was running. She could hear Thalia arguing shrilly with her mother behind their closed door. "But what about me? But what about me? What am I supposed to do?"

Ellen tossed her coat and hat on the chair in the corner that was already heaped with clothes. Ma must have been too busy to straighten up that day. Or she was not feeling well again. How many times had she seen her mixing a spoonful of that brown tonic in a glass of water and drinking it down? Too many. Ellen lay down on her rumpled bed and closed her burning eyes.

I have been such a fool, she thought. I'm a boarding-house Irish girl with no prospects for anything that I don't earn myself. I'll never be invited to watch a polo match. I'll never see Hawaii or New York or Paris, or even Lake Tahoe. I'll be a shop girl until I'm so old that I can't stand on my feet anymore.

Or else I'll end up married to one of the McCarthys, with a dozen children following me round the house yelling, "Ma! Ma!" And I'll end up a widow like my own ma, running a boardinghouse to keep from starving, and I'll watch my daughters making the same mistakes I did. The idea made her cry.

She rolled over on her stomach and thought, I just managed to break two promises at the same time. I must still care about being a part of the "right" crowd, or I wouldn't be bawling about it. And I'm giving up on the idea of the shop being successful enough to get me everything I really want.

A few minutes later, she heard Mary Clare bellowing from the foot of the stairs, "Dinner, everybody. Dinner."

Somewhere in San Francisco, families were being summoned calmly to their dining rooms by butlers or maids. She had Mary Clare, with her hair coming down in a tangle and gravy spots on her apron. Ellen sat up, smoothed her own hair, and went downstairs with a carefully arranged smile on her face.

As Mary Clare had said once when she burned her hand, "Didn't my gran always tell us that life hurts, but at least it's short? Being dead will take up a much longer time." Ellen was laughing when she entered the dining room.

On Friday, Ellen sold the first dress in the shop. Until that time, she had had to struggle with the specter of failure that seemed to grow more distinct every day. They had few customers, and some women bought nothing at all. But on

Friday a friend of Kate's came in, a girl with thick glasses and flawless white skin. After greeting Kate, she looked around without comment until she saw the pink dress hanging on the wall opposite the counter.

"It's charming, Kate," she said. She turned up the hem and examined the stitches. "Beautiful work," she murmured.

Kate took down the dress. "Ellen made it. Did you notice the wonderful neckline? The collar is flat and comfortable. Would you like to try it on?" she asked. Ellen expected the girl to decline.

"I would." The girl looked around. "Where can I go?"

"We have a changing room," Kate explained. "It's rather small, but . . ."

The girl smiled. "I'm sure that will be fine. Aren't you brave, taking on a shop? I'd tell Mama, but you know how she is about girls going out on their own. She might think I wanted to try it."

Kate showed her the way to the little dressing room. The girl declined help, so Kate hurried back out to the shop to whisper, "I can't believe this." The dress was expensive because of the delicate fabric, and Ellen was afraid that the girl might not be able to afford it.

Kate grinned and held a finger to her lips.

Fifteen minutes later, Kate was packing the dress in tissue paper and sliding it into one of the blue paper boxes. The girl left with it, smiling. Outside, a young man stepped out from the door of the tobacco shop next door and walked off beside her.

"Who was that?" Ellen asked.

Kate, marking the sale on a sheet of paper the way Aunt Grace had said that they must, said, "Jane Vert. She lives across the street from the Logan house. I have a hunch she's not supposed to be seeing that boy—she's too young. Mrs. Vert would go crazy if she found out, because she had always planned on trotting Jane around Europe in a few years, with the hope that she would land a man with a title."

"Like Milly Goodrich?" Ellen asked. Milly Goodrich was one of the little girls going into the hotel so many years before. "Or should I say Lady Mildred?"

"Not where your mother can hear you," Kate said, laughing. "You know how she hates to hear about American girls marrying old men and coming home for a visit and expecting everyone to curtsey."

"Women curtsey, men bow," Ellen supplied.

"Tell that to your mother," Kate said, grinning.

"Not if I want to live."

Kate consulted the small blue enameled clock on the shelf behind her. "Do you want to take the first lunch?"

"I thought you would."

"You're not meeting anyone, are you?" Kate asked. Her expression looked innocent enough, but her green eyes were suspicious. Obviously she was still worrying about

Aaron. Aaron, who had never called Ellen after that Saturday.

That Saturday. The end of the world. The grim, nearly empty cabin that smelled of mold and dust. The final sickening understanding that no one else was coming. Aaron's confident, smiling suggestion, while his damp hand cupped her chin. Her own red rage at him. At herself! The endless, furious, heartbreaking walk in tight shoes along a rutted dirt road, until an old woman in a wagon gave her a ride.

Ellen was not in the mood to be nagged by Kate. "Hugh said he might stop by the tearoom around the corner, if he had time."

"All right, then."

"You're offending me, Kate!" Ellen blurted.

"Sorry!" Kate said. "You know I wouldn't do that. But you also know why I'm worrying. You haven't mentioned Aaron since I told you he'd been in here, and I haven't been sure how you felt."

"If you think I'm wasting away with love for him, you're mistaken," Ellen said stiffly. "I never felt that way about him. There just was a time when I thought . . . Never mind."

Oh, to be as independent and self-confident as this red-haired girl who had had the courage to take on an invalid and a trip halfway around the world. Opening a shop was an adventure to Kate. So was assuming the responsibility for an elderly relative. Kate knew what she wanted and how to get it. And she did not make mistakes. And she would never allow a man to make a mistake about *her*.

Just before Ellen took off her apron to leave for lunch, the door opened again, and this time Aaron Schuster came in. Ellen's heart seemed to lurch. She was not ready to see him yet. He was with his sister, whom Ellen recognized from all the newspaper photographs she had seen. Ellen found a certain satisfaction in noting that she was not so good looking as she had thought. Her thin nose looked like a bird's beak, and her forehead was too high. Her chilly smile did not extend to her eyes when Aaron introduced Ellen to her, and she said nothing, turning immediately, silk skirt rustling, to look at the goods displayed on the shelves. Her colorless eyebrows raised, and she shook her head a little, just a little, as if what she saw amused her.

"We're on our way to Grandmother's for an early lunch, and I thought we'd stop by and see how you're doing. You weren't here when we came before. Are you excited, having your own place? Are you already planning on expanding to Los Angeles and maybe even New York?" He laughed nervously—and made the mistake of looking to Kate for support and approval. Kate calmly turned her back and walked away.

Ellen smiled, but she was furious, both from embarrassment at his presence and anger at what she perceived to be mockery of the shop. "We're too busy here to make plans for anything else for a long time," she said, hoping that this would turn out to be true.

Miss Schuster walked toward the door without saying a word to her brother or to Ellen. What arrogance! She was halfway out before Aaron realized she was leaving, and he sprang after her, shocked and laughing. "She always gets her own way!" he shouted. "Good-bye!" The door closed.

"Lovely," Kate muttered disgustedly. "And those are the people you think are worth knowing."

"Well, I *did,*" Ellen said. "She's awfully spoiled," she added, as if that was an excuse for the sister's rudeness.

Kate snorted. "You'd better hurry to meet Hugh. He's probably waiting."

Ellen looked forward to having lunch with her brother, especially after the unsatisfactory visit from Aaron. Oh, if he had only stayed away! She did not want to think about him. She took off her apron, put on her hat, and paused at the door.

"You know, we have the prettiest window on the street," she said, in an effort to change Kate's disgusted expression.

"Not hard, when we're keeping company with a tobacco shop, a bookstore, and Petrillo's Cheap Shoe Repairs," Kate said. She rewarded Ellen with a smile.

Ellen ran off, and found Hugh waiting impatiently for her. But she repeated Kate's description of the windows on their block, and he cheered up.

"Kate is a wonder," he said. "Nothing ever discourages her."

Ellen smiled to herself. Let Adele do her best to charm her brother. Kate would always be his favorite.

Time took on a kind of order that became oddly soothing. Ellen spent her days in the shop, exchanged smiles with Kate over every customer, and went home again to dinner in the boardinghouse with Ma and the others, only to start all over the next morning, except for the weekends.

One Saturday evening, she went with Germaine to a play, and Hugh met her afterward and took her home. The next Saturday evening, Matt McCarthy celebrated his birthday in a restaurant, and Ellen was there, along with two dozen other young people. Kate came, too. And Adele, who was Hugh's guest. Ellen's only satisfaction there was that Hugh took Kate home also.

She did her best to concentrate on one day at a time, pushing away worries—and memories that were uncomfortable. After all, what could she do about them? Her mother had told her a hundred times that joy was to be found in small things, but Ellen had not yet reached the point where she found that to be true. Small things—the loud voices in the boardinghouse, the food smells that lingered in the halls, the broken corset lace she discovered at the last moment—exasperated her. The big things—Joe running with a gang, the leak in the ceiling of the third-floor hall, Ma's loss of weight, that occurrence with Aaron—kept her awake at night.

Then one day she read in a newspaper that Aaron, his sister, and their grandmother had left San Francisco for a month of boating on Puget Sound. Several friends would be joining them for the last two weeks, before they all returned for a round of summer parties. "I hope the boat sinks," Ellen muttered. Later, she dropped the newspaper into the box of kindling behind the kitchen stove. Upstairs in her bedroom, she looked out the window for a long time.

Then, on a particularly foggy Thursday morning, Ma said, "Happy birthday, Ellen! You forgot all about it, didn't you?" Ellen, shocked, realized that she was another year older—twenty now!—and she covered her face and cried. For a moment, Ma, Mary Clare, and Thalia laughed, teasing her. But she could not stop weeping for several minutes, and then only when Ma poured her a cup of tea and put four teaspoons of sugar in it.

"Drink it down as fast as you can," Ma said. "And wipe your eyes. It's not as if you're forty!"

"But you do have little wrinkles at the corners of your eyes," Thalia said sympathetically. "I'm sorry, Ellen."

They all laughed, then, and Ellen drank her too-sweet tea. They would make her a birthday cake during the day, and she would share it with the boarders. Just as she always did. Always and forever. It was a sober thought.

Kate left the shop halfway through the morning, to go to Chinatown for more of the blue boxes they used. Miss Keely was busy in the back room with her account book. Ellen looked up when she heard the shop door open, hoping it would not be someone who only wanted to ask questions about the linen goods. She was in no mood to talk.

It was Mr. Woodmark. Ellen nodded in response to his "Good morning," then busied herself with rearranging the pillowcases. He paused at Kate's newest creation, a navy blue dress with a sailor collar, which hung from a hook on the wall across from the counter.

"Please tell me that this dress does not have . . . hmm . . ." He paused and stroked his small, neat beard with one finger. Then, suddenly, he turned to Ellen. "Trousers? The dress has *trousers* instead of a skirt?"

Ellen could have slapped him quite cheerfully. She had hated Kate's idea of a bicycling costume, but Kate had gone ahead and made it anyway. And it was not all that bad. One could scarcely tell that the skirt was divided down the middle, like trousers, because it was full and pleated.

"That is a bicycling costume," Ellen said stiffly. "Some women wear them. The college girls. When they go bicycling." She hated herself for trying to explain.

"Ah," Mr. Woodmark said, bending forward to peer at

the dress again. "I see." He turned back to Ellen then and asked, "Is Miss Keely here? The young Miss Keely?"

"Miss Keely is out for a while," Ellen said. "May I help you with something?" She hoped that the ice in her voice would discourage any response from him except, "No, thank you."

The insufferable man would not take a hint. "No, I really want to talk to her," he said. "Will you ask her to get in touch with me?"

"Where?" Ellen asked.

He seemed bewildered by her question. "Why, where else? My flat is right upstairs."

"I cannot give her a message like that," Ellen said. "But I am sure that Miss Keely would be happy to keep an appointment with you here, in the shop, or *with her aunt* in your flat."

"Good lord," Mr. Woodmark said. "What are you implying?"

"What are *you* implying?" Ellen asked.

Mr. Woodmark blinked behind his glasses. "Would you allow me to write her a note? Or should I write a formal letter and send it through the post? Or have it delivered by a priest? Or better yet, a nun?"

Ellen opened her mouth to deliver what she hoped would be a crushing remark, but Kate ran in, breathless and flushed, her arms filled with folded boxes.

"Hello there!" she said to Mr. Woodmark. "What a nice surprise."

"Apparently not," he said, glancing sideways at Ellen. "However, if it's all right with the police, I would like to have a word with you on a small business matter."

Kate looked baffled for a moment, but then smiled. "Come with me to the storeroom. Aunt's back there, and I'm sure that you'll want to talk to her, too."

"She's here? I wouldn't have bothered you if I had known *she* was here. But of course, it might not be proper for me to go behind a curtain with two unwed ladies."

"Oh, for heaven's sake!" Ellen cried. She turned her back and busied herself rearranging folded pillowcases. Kate's laughter did not help. She and Mr. Woodmark went behind the curtain, and Ellen could hear Kate's aunt say, "I thought I heard you out there!"

Wretched man. He certainly was wealthy enough to live an exciting life in San Francisco, but as far as Ellen could determine, he spent his time grubbing about in the bookstore up the street or meeting with the steady stream of nondescript guests who climbed the stairs to his flat during the day. What a bore!

And then she remembered Aaron and that last stupid, stupid Saturday, and her eyes burned as if they were filled with sand.

After Mr. Woodmark left, Ellen asked Kate what he had wanted. She was prepared to disapprove of anything.

"There is a small storeroom upstairs and he wondered if we'd like to rent it, since ours isn't very large." Kate stacked unfolded boxes under the counter and then straightened up. "Aunt said we'd have to think about it."

"Aren't we expecting more linen goods? Maybe we need extra space."

"We won't be getting so much that we can't keep it in back. And every penny counts now. Aunt knows more about how much stock we should keep on hand, so I'll let her decide."

"He should have sent a note," Ellen said.

"What on earth is wrong with you?" Kate demanded. "You're acting as if you don't want him coming into the shop. Men have been in here, and it's not as if he was pawing through our goods."

"But he was!" Ellen said. "Well, almost. He made some rude remarks about your bicycling dress."

Kate stared at her. "What rude remarks? What was going on?"

"He noticed right away that the dress doesn't have a skirt."

"Well, it doesn't! Exactly what did he say that upset you so much?"

Ellen sighed. "All right, it wasn't so much what he said but how he said it."

"Men are peculiar," Kate said. "You know that. You can't expect them to accept a new idea right away."

"And what do *you* know about men, Kate?" Ellen said. She was laughing now.

"More than I ever wanted to learn, thanks to my stay in your mother's boardinghouse. Now, shall we change the window display? I was thinking that we might tie a blue ribbon around half a dozen folded sheets and put the stack next to the painting and then unfold an embroidered sheet on the floor so that the decoration shows."

"We could put a few paper flowers on it," Ellen suggested.

Peace had been restored. They had almost had a quarrel, and over that insufferable bearded puppy, Woodmark!

Ellen went home to what she hoped would be a quiet evening, but instead, she was greeted at the boardinghouse door with a noisy quarrel that had been going on for some time, apparently.

Her mother, red-faced, hands on hips, was saying, "I will not cut the rent by three-quarters, just because you are leaving that girl here again. If she stays in the big room, you pay full price. Otherwise, she stays on the third floor, and I will not keep the big room available to you. I've had enough of this."

Mr. Rutledge, dressed in a striped suit and looking more like a professional gambler than anything else, slapped his hat against his leg and said, "I expect accommodation from you in this matter, because we have paid you a great deal of money in the past and probably will do so in the future."

"This is *my* house," Ma began, and then she gasped and clenched her hands together tightly. For a moment she was silent, but then she said, "Pack up Thalia's clothes and take her with you. I won't have a child left here alone, for me to care for and worry about, when I don't even know where you are going."

"We can't do that! She'll be going back to school in September, and we don't want her education interrupted."

"You don't mind interrupting that boy's life! You're dragging him all over the country like a circus freak!"

Mr. Rutledge took out his pocket watch and consulted it with a melodramatic sigh. "I don't have time to discuss this with you. Put Thalia back on the third floor and I'll give you enough money to keep her for two months. But I will expect accommodation—"

"If you say 'accommodation' one more time, I'll accommodate you with my foot on the seat of your pants!" Ma shouted.

Ellen put her hand on her mother's arm. Ma's color was unhealthy, and she clenched her hands even more tightly until her knuckles were white. "Ma, never mind. I'll settle this. You go on and see to dinner."

Her mother stumbled away, and Ellen caught a look of triumph on Mr. Rutledge's face.

"Don't think you've won," she said crisply. "I made it

my business to consult a lawyer about your abandoning Thalia before. I can have you jailed."

She had not consulted a lawyer, but she had correctly read Rutledge's desire to avoid trouble on this day. He was in a hurry to take his wife and son somewhere, so let him pay for Thalia's stay in the boardinghouse.

"Give me the rent, and she'll need money for clothes, too," Ellen said. "We gave them to her last time. And money for the doctor if she gets sick. And for school fees."

"*Whaaat?*" Mr. Rutledge howled. "What's going on here?"

Ellen held out her hand. "Pay me now. Two months' rent on the small room, plus ten dollars for her clothes and medical care. And two dollars for books and school fees."

Mr. Rutledge pulled a roll of paper money out of his pocket and peeled off enough to pay the rent. "I'll send the rest to you," he said, and before Ellen could stop him, he turned his back and began shouting for his wife and son.

They hurried down, as if they had been eavesdropping on the landing, and as the boy passed, Ellen saw that his mother had burned his ear with the crimping iron again, leaving a red blister. The boy saw her sympathetic look and responded with a scowl.

Thalia was nowhere in sight.

After the Rutledges left, Ellen went to look for the girl. She was moving her few dresses upstairs to the small bedroom. Her eyelids were swollen from weeping, and when she saw Ellen coming, she turned her face away.

"It will be all right," Ellen said. "You'll see."

Thalia stopped two steps from the top and looked back at Ellen. "They said I can quit school when I'm fourteen, and they'll find me a job. I'll be able to pay for my own room then."

Ellen wanted to scream aloud, to run after the Rutledges and pound sense into them, to make them take their daughter with them and give her a stable life. But she hurried ahead of Thalia and opened the door to the small room.

"I'm glad you'll be staying with us," she said.

Thalia only nodded.

Ellen ran downstairs to see about her mother then, and found her sitting at the table with a cup of tea before her, one hand pressed against her stomach.

"Ma, what's wrong? I could tell you were in pain."

Ma took another sip of tea, then said, "I had to clench my hands because it doesn't look right for a woman to put her hand on her stomach."

Ellen blinked. "What are you talking about?"

"I've got some kind of woman trouble, and I needed to 'sorry' it." She rubbed one side of her stomach to remind Ellen of the times when she would 'sorry' the small injuries and pains that afflicted her children from time to time.

"But I didn't want that man to see me put my hand on my stomach. We don't look strong to men when they think we have trouble of some kind, especially women's trouble. And don't you forget it!"

Ellen was ready to laugh, but her mother looked so ill. She glanced quickly at Mary Clare and caught her concerned expression just before she smiled. "Your ma's probably just going through the change," she said.

"That's right," Ma said. "You have to expect a few aches and pains then."

Ellen had no idea what a woman might expect in middle age, but she was willing to believe anything, as long as it was not serious news.

"I'll run up and change clothes, and then I'll help Mary Clare get dinner on the table for the boarders," she said. "You just sit there and tell us what to do."

She had not expected her mother to obey, but she did. Ellen ran for the stairs.

Ma will be all right. Nobody has *that* much bad luck, she told herself. She pulled a plain cotton dress from the wardrobe and began changing clothes.

Nothing's wrong with her.

Chapter 11
KATE

Several of the girls from Adele's typing class came in the shop one Saturday, and their delight raised Kate's spirits. All left with blue boxes. One promised to tell her cousin, a university student, about The Water Lily, and Kate repeated the comment to Ellen.

"You're still hoping to sell your bicycling costume," Ellen said, shaking her head. "I'll have to see it happen before I believe it."

"Trousers are catching on," Kate said. "Aunt says she's seen them—well, two or three—in the department stores."

"Who would buy one?" Ellen asked. "I wouldn't. But I'll keep my fingers crossed that the shop catches on with college girls. They like nice things, and if one of them has something, all the rest want it, too."

"It's the same with the working Irish girls," Kate said. "I keep hoping we'll see them here, too. Don't they like what we're selling?" She sighed. "Is it the linen, or is it us?"

"Perhaps both. Linen might be too 'Irish.' And they're not impressed with two more working Irish girls, since Irish women always seem to be working. But listen, Kate. Last Sunday the priest said all young women are supposed to marry, or else find jobs and help their parents if they aren't called to be nuns. On the way home, I told Ma that he should come up with a cheery message like that for the men, but she said men don't go to mass so often, and anyway he wouldn't think that they needed to be told anything. It's just us females who are so ignorant." Ellen sighed and rubbed her forehead as if she had a headache. "Why is life so unfair? Sometimes I could just scream."

Kate, rearranging petticoats on shelves, said, "The men in the village in Ireland didn't like the factory. They didn't like seeing the women working there, even though none of the women was married. Jolie's aunt was careful to only hire old maids and widows, just so she could avoid trouble with the men."

"She never hired men?"

"No, and I can't imagine a man wanting to make women's underwear. Sheets and tablecloths, maybe. But most of the men didn't work at all. Times are very hard there. There's nothing for them to do. It isn't really their fault, and I suppose the factory reminds them of what they can't have—jobs."

"They should come to San Francisco," Ellen said.

"Everybody's working here. And that's why Hugh says we're sure to be a big success."

"I don't know about 'big,'" Kate said. "But I appreciate his thought."

"But do you appreciate *him*?" Ellen asked.

Kate was startled by the question. "Of course I appreciate Hugh!" she said. "What would we have done without him when we were getting the shop ready? Or when Aunt and I were moving into our flat? He did more than anyone else, getting us settled. I adore your brother."

"Perhaps you don't 'adore' him in the right way," Ellen said. She avoided looking at Kate, but Kate read her mind anyway.

"Hugh is like my brother," she said. "And he is fond of Adele, who is perfect for him. She has his sense of humor—and both of them eat clams, which I hate."

Ellen shook her head a little. "Ah, Kate, at least you could give him a chance. I see how he looks at you when you're not watching. And he's grown to be such a good man. I don't know what we'd do without him, especially since Joe is turning into such a young devil. Hugh would be so good to you."

Kate could not believe what she was hearing. "Ellen, what's gotten into you? You know I can't afford to have . . . have feelings for any man. I've got Aunt to care for, for the rest of her life. What man would want to help with that responsibility?"

"Hugh would," Ellen said firmly. "I know he would. He'd even let you go on working in the shop."

Kate stopped folding petticoats. "Oh, please tell me that you haven't had this discussion with Hugh! I'd die of embarrassment. What you're hinting at will never happen, Ellen. It won't! I'll never be serious about a man, at least not for a very long time. And by that time Hugh will have settled down in a house near his cove and have four children—and clams for dinner every night."

Ellen's eyes filled with tears, and she turned her back on Kate. Kate reached out and touched her shoulder. "What's wrong? Surely you didn't have your heart set on it? You've always known how I felt about my duty to my aunt, and you've known all my plans. When did I ever say I wanted the life that most women have? Why Ellen, you don't want to marry, either, at least until you're thirty. I've heard you say it a thousand times."

"Not even then," Ellen said, and she invented a reason to go to the storeroom. Aunt was not there that morning, and Kate wondered if Ellen needed someone to talk to, but the door opened then and two women came in to look at sheets.

Long after they left, carrying boxes, Ellen came back in the shop, her eyes red. But she was smiling ruefully.

"I'm sorry, Kate. Ma's been sick, and Mary Clare and I are trying to cope, and I guess I'm just worrying about everything these days."

"What's wrong with your mother?" Kate asked, alarmed. "This is the first I've heard of it."

"She thought she had some kind of woman's trouble, but the doctor said it could be her appendix. She might need to have it taken out, but she'll argue about it. She worries about how the boarders will get along—and so do I. Everything happens at once, doesn't it? Joe's no help, either. He's running with a bunch of boys who'll end up in jail, Ma says. The worry isn't doing her any good at all."

A shiver ran up Kate's arms. "Maybe she should see another doctor. They don't always agree on things. There might be a medication she could take that would ease things."

"I told her that, but she's going to the doctor that Mrs. Stackhouse has been seeing lately, and he's supposed to be the best one in San Francisco."

"Oh, everything Mrs. Stackhouse has or does or thinks or says is supposed to be the best!" Kate said disgustedly. "Is your mother in pain all the time?"

"I think so, but you know she'd never admit it."

This was not good. Mrs. Flannery was the kind of woman—and mother—who would sacrifice her own health while she was caring for someone else. And being the keeper of a large, noisy boardinghouse had brought her more pleasure than Kate could understand.

"Ma drives me crazy sometimes," Ellen went on, frowning. "But I don't know what I'd do if something happened to her. I never thought I'd see the day that Ma would miss going to morning mass, but she's just too sick sometimes."

"Nothing will happen to her," Kate said. Mrs. Flannery's illness worried her, but now she was worried about Ellen, too. What would she do if her mother became so sick that she could not manage the boardinghouse? The responsibility would fall on Ellen, who would hate it as much as Kate would.

Could Hugh help at a time like that? He meant well, but Kate could not see him taking over any of the boardinghouse responsibilities. Probably he would not even see what needed to be done. A curious kind of unawareness seemed to affect most men.

As if summoned, Mr. Woodmark came in the shop, looking somewhat bemused. But that seemed to be his ordinary expression, Kate thought, smiling to herself.

"Good grief," Ellen muttered. "Here comes the petticoat police."

"Hello!" Kate called out, more to drown out Ellen than because she was always happy to see Mr. Woodmark. He was a nice man, but lately his occasional visits unnerved her. She worried that he might find something about the shop that was unacceptable, therefore in violation of her lease. She wanted to appear successful in his eyes—and old enough to manage the shop.

He seemed uncomfortable, and he looked everywhere

except at Kate's face. "I've come to invite you to a picnic three weeks from Sunday at my family's place on the ocean," he said. "We've done this every year for—I don't know how long. Years!—and all the shop people in this building, and the people who work on *High Tide*, come and bring family and guests. Everyone seems to have a good time." He waited, apparently for an answer.

Ellen stared.

Kate flushed and said, "That's very nice of you. Where is this place?"

"Ah," Mr. Woodmark said. "It's across the Bay. I'll arrange for transportation for everybody. We'll pick you up when you get off the ferry and have you at the house in no time."

Ellen made a small, strangled sound. Kate turned to look at her, but Ellen shook her head. Her mouth was a tight line.

Kate hesitated, then said, "I'll ask my aunt and let you know."

"I hope you'll come," he said earnestly. "Your aunt would enjoy herself. *High Tide* hasn't been published since the quake, but we're bringing out an issue in a few months, so this is an exciting time for us and we're in a mood to celebrate. And you know the shop people here in the building, don't you? So the more people who come, the better it will be."

"I couldn't possibly go," Ellen said stiffly.

"Hugh would love it!" Kate said. "You know how he enjoys a day at the ocean. He could bring Adele—"

"By all means!" Mr. Woodmark said. "Bring anyone you like."

Kate was more pleased than she cared to show, but she assured him that she would ask Aunt and tell him in plenty of time if they were going. After he left, Kate turned to Ellen and said, "Don't you want to go? Surely you don't dislike him that much."

But Ellen had pressed a shaking hand over her eyes. "Kate, I'm worried about Ma. I have to go home and check on things. Can you manage the shop alone this afternoon?"

"Go home right now," Kate said, concerned.

"And, Kate," Ellen said, "please don't go alone to this man's picnic—or whatever he wants to call it. You don't know if he's telling the truth and—"

"Ellen!" Kate exclaimed. "What are you talking about? Of course I wouldn't go without Aunt."

Ellen blinked, then said, "I worry about you. You're still so trusting, so sure that everybody means you well. Not everyone does, you know."

"Don't fuss," Kate said firmly. "Now run home. And send Joe with word if I can help you. I'll come by after work."

Ellen left, forgetting to remove her apron, and Kate watched her fly past the window. Mrs. Flannery had to be all right. It was impossible to imagine the world without the strong, practical woman.

For half an hour the shop was empty, and then, to Kate's astonishment, Dr. Logan came in. He glanced around and then said, "Isn't your aunt here? I'd hoped to see her, too."

"She's home," Kate said. "I'm sure she'd be glad to see you."

"She wasn't there when I stopped by," he said. He seemed even more exhausted than he had the last time she had seen him, and even more worried. "I really need to talk to you both. And Miss Flannery, too."

"I'm the only one here," Kate said, beginning to feel alarmed. "What's wrong? Why are you back in San Francisco?"

But before he could answer, three women came into the shop, smiling and curious about the dresses hanging on the wall.

Dr. Logan held up one hand. "I'm disturbing your business," he said, lowering his voice. "I'll visit a friend upstairs for a few minutes and then come back. I know Mr. Woodmark."

"You do?" Kate asked, surprised.

"Oh, yes. After he recovered from the injuries he received on his trip home last December, his doctor sent me a medical history, but I had stopped practicing by then, so I arranged for Woodmark to see a colleague of mine for his follow-up care."

"What injuries?" Kate asked, amazed. She glanced at her customers, who were examining the seams in the dresses, and then whispered, "He seems just fine."

"He had been attacked by robbers on a train," Dr. Logan murmured. "Can you imagine such a thing? I thought those bad days were gone forever. No, the thieves came aboard the train at a meal stop, and Woodmark and some other men defended the passengers. He was badly injured, and he was taken to the home of a doctor I know."

"What train? When?" Kate asked.

"Around Christmastime," Dr. Logan said. "Has he told you about it? I suppose he has."

"Not a word," Kate said. She glanced at her customers again. One had taken down the dark blue linen dress and was holding it up to one of her friends.

"You're busy," Dr. Logan said. "I shouldn't take up your time. But Kate . . . " He paused and looked down for a moment. "Kate, I saw Jolie's watercolor in your window. You'll never know what that means to me. The watercolor and the name of the shop . . . Jolie would have been so pleased. Now I'll go upstairs and see if Woodmark is home. I'll come back in a few minutes."

The journal, Kate thought, watching him go. It was written by Mr. Woodmark. It must have been. It had fallen out of his pocket when he was taken off the train.

"We have a place in back where you can try that on," she said to her customer.

While one tried on the dress, the other two went through a dozen petticoats and each chose two. "I love these things," one said. "We heard about the place. You're practically famous, you know. All the girls at college are talking about you."

I wish it were true, Kate thought, even as she smiled.

The young women had been gone for ten minutes before Dr. Logan came back. "I enjoyed my visit with Woodmark," he said. "He's glad to have you as his tenant. But I didn't discuss your business with him. I don't have very good news, I'm afraid."

"I don't understand," Kate said. What bad news could Dr. Logan have that concerned her shop?

He reached inside his coat for an envelope. "I've had a distressing letter from Jolie's aunt. About the factory."

"What's happened?" Kate asked quickly. "We haven't received our order yet—it's late—and I've begun to worry."

He shook his head. "I have no news about that, but you won't be getting anything else from the factory," he said. "It was destroyed. My sister-in-law wrote that it had been set on fire by some of the men from the village. Here, let me read what she said."

He unfolded the letter with trembling fingers while Kate waited, listening to her heart beat hard in her chest. "Here it is:

> "I'm sorry to say that the men have always hated us, and now they've had their revenge. The factory was destroyed by fire last week, along with everything in it. At least they had the decency to burn us out at night when the women were not there. I don't have the heart to rebuild. We've battled the prejudice against us and our ideas for too many years. I have wanted to make my permanent home in Italy for a long time, so now I feel free to do it. Please explain to Kate that we can't supply her needs and tell her that I am more sorry that I can express. I'll write to her myself when I can bear to give her the details. Right now my failure is too painful."

Kate pressed her fingers against her lips while he refolded the letter and put it back in his inside pocket.

"That's it?" she asked finally. She was afraid her tongue would stick to the roof of her dry mouth if she said anything more.

Dr. Logan nodded soberly. "I'm afraid that it is. I know she'll write to you herself—she is a woman of her word. I believe that she is heartbroken over this. The factory that she and her husband built was a source of great pride to her. They did so much for the women in the village. But I think you must find another supplier for your goods. The factory is finished."

"Thank you for telling me," she said. "I'll write to her

and let her know that you've told me. I do want the details. Perhaps I can deal directly with the women who worked there. Some of them surely want to continue."

"Don't count on it," he said sadly. "It's never easy for people to go against their community. My sister-in-law and her husband were brave people. But she's old now and not very well—she'll be happy in Italy."

Kate nodded. She remembered the fondness Jolie's aunt had always expressed for Italy. She had wanted to take Jolie there, too.

Dr. Logan left, and Kate refolded the petticoats that had not been sold. She could not order her thoughts. What would they do if the delayed shipment never arrived? She and Ellen had counted on selling linens forever. The two of them could not sew enough to keep the shop open, even if they could find cloth of good enough quality at a price they could afford. They would have to find people to sew.

They might lose The Water Lily. And their hope of independence.

As soon as she closed the shop, she hurried to the Flannery boardinghouse. Mary Clare and Thalia were in the kitchen, putting together a skimpy dinner that would be sure to disappoint the boarders. Mary Clare said that Mrs. Flannery was lying down in her room and Ellen was making up the bedrooms, since there had not been enough time for Mary Clare to do all the work.

"And do you think that them lazy boarders would lift a finger to help, even if Our Lady Herself was here and looking for a place to rest?" Mary Clare complained as she slammed pans around on the stove.

"Or carry a plate back to the kitchen?" Thalia said in a voice remarkably like Mary Clare's whine. She had slopped dishwater down the front of her dress and Kate saw, incongruously, that she was wearing odd socks. Thalia's glance followed hers. "I hardly had any time to get dressed this morning," she complained, "and I didn't notice that I had on a blue sock and a black sock. But Joe says odd socks are lucky."

Kate held up her hands in protest. "It's all right. Give me a chance to run upstairs and see how Mrs. Flannery is doing, and then I'll come down and help out."

"Oh, it would be such a blessing if you would!" Mary Clare cried. Kate fled before the cook began weeping.

She found Mrs. Flannery awake in her room, flushed with fever and breathing heavily, her rosary beads clicking in her fingers. Kate pulled the chair close to the bed.

"How are you? And tell me the truth," Kate said.

Mrs. Flannery wrapped her rosary around one hand, then propped herself up on one elbow. "I'm better than I was a while ago," she said. "But Ellen and Hugh won't let me get up. Hugh's gone to find Joe. I'm so worried. I haven't seen the boy since after breakfast this morning, and I can't get any rest until I know he's all right."

"I'll bring you a cup of tea, and then I'll help Mary Clare get dinner on the table for the boarders," Kate said, removing her hat. "Don't move. And when Joe gets home, I'm going to give him such a smack that he'll remember it for the rest of his life."

"You don't fool me, Kate," Mrs. Flannery said, laughing weakly. "You won't smack him."

"I will!" Kate said, and she hurried away.

She might not smack Joe, but she planned on having a word with him when he got home. He always was in awe of her. But dinner was on the table before Hugh came home, and he was alone. Kate took him out to the hall for a private conversation.

"I couldn't find Joe anywhere," Hugh said. "I went around to all his friends, but they say they haven't seen him—or they're lying. Either way, I hate to tell Ma that I failed."

Kate put her hand on his arm. "Ellen looked in on her a while ago and said she was asleep. Let's let her rest for as long as she can. Joe will probably come home on his own, once he thinks he's gotten all he can out of creating this big fuss."

But Hugh looked worried. "Drat him. This is no time for him to be acting like this. He used to mind me when I got tough enough, but lately I can't control him at all. Ma frets over him, and I wouldn't be surprised that he's making her feel worse. Adele says he'll behave better once school starts again in the fall, but he wasn't doing very well before."

So Hugh discussed his family with Adele. Good. Ellen might not realize it, but Adele was going to be part of the Flannery family's future.

Dinner was over and the boarders had gone their separate ways when the doorbell rang. Kate answered it—Ellen was helping in the kitchen, and Hugh had gone out again to search for Joe.

Two policemen stood there. "Are you related to Joseph Flannery?" the tall one asked. "A sister?"

"I'm a friend of the family," she said. She pressed her hands against her chest, as if she could guard her heart from what was coming. "What's happened?"

"We need to speak to a family member," the policeman said. He was firm, but she saw pity in his eyes.

"Joe's mother is ill and resting in bed," Kate said. "I'll get his sister."

She turned to run upstairs, but Ellen was standing there, hands clapped over her mouth. And behind her, halfway down the stairs, Mrs. Flannery stood frozen.

"Come in," Kate said to the policemen. "We'll hear your news inside."

The tall policeman gave the news quickly. Joe had been badly injured, half buried while he was playing on a construction site, and he lay in a hospital.

"Is he dying?" his mother asked hoarsely.

"We'll take you to the hospital, missus," the policeman said by way of answer, and Mrs. Flannery nodded.

"I'll get our coats," Ellen said. "Somebody can send Hugh when he gets home."

"I'm coming, too," Kate said.

Behind them, a few of the boarders had gathered silently in the hall. But halfway up the stairs, Thalia was weeping.

Joe lay on a bed in a long ward, surrounded by screens. The doctors had given him something to ease his pain, and he barely spoke when he saw his mother and sister. Both of his legs had been broken, and one hand was wrapped in a bandage. A nurse scurried away and returned with a doctor, who explained that Joe's legs had been so badly shattered that surgery would be required to mend them.

"I'm just glad he's alive," Mrs. Flannery said.

But Kate had seen something flicker in the doctor's eyes when he mentioned surgery. He doesn't think Joe will be able to walk again, she thought, sickened. It was not her place to ask questions, but Mrs. Flannery's questions were not about walking. They were about when her boy could come home again.

"It might be a long time," the doctor said. "We'll have to see about that. And now you must let him rest. We'll talk again tomorrow."

Hugh arrived then, greeted his drowsy brother with a

mild scolding for worrying everybody, and then took his mother's arm. "I've borrowed an auto," he said. "Let's go so Joe can sleep. I'll bring you back tomorrow, first thing, Ma."

Reluctantly, Mrs. Flannery left. As she walked down the hospital halls, she held her hand pressed against her side, and Kate was close to panic. She's so ill, she thought. Somebody has to make her get the care she needs.

But later, in the warm kitchen at the boardinghouse, Mrs. Flannery refused to consider seeing a doctor. When Kate left, she was setting oatmeal to soak for breakfast.

Hugh walked Kate home in the dark. He did not speak until they reached the door of the flat, and then he said, "I'll try to get Ma to a doctor tomorrow. And you'll have to do without Ellen in the shop for a while, until we get everything sorted out at home."

"Don't worry about it," Kate said. "I can handle everything. Just tell Ellen . . ."

But Hugh turned and ran down the steps without waiting for her message, and Kate let herself in the door where Aunt waited.

Joe's first surgery was performed the following day, another a few days later, and still no one could predict whether the boy would ever use his legs again. Mrs. Flannery spent her days sitting by his bed and her nights working in the boardinghouse, until Ellen found her unconscious in their room one morning. She had surgery in another hospital that afternoon—but she died without waking up.

Aunt had been sitting with Joe that day, reassuring him that his mother would be fine in a few days and back beside his bed again. "But," she told Kate later, "at about two-thirty, the boy said, 'Ma! Please don't!' Why, you'd have thought he was seeing her walking out the door. And when Hugh came, he told the boy that was when his mother died. Two-thirty exactly. Now what do you think of that, Kate?"

Kate put down her cup of tea. "I think she came to say good-bye, Aunt."

Mrs. Flannery was buried on Thursday. Ellen and Hugh, dressed in new black, stood close together, and Hugh held his sister's hand tightly in his own. Adele clung to his other arm, her eyes wet with tears.

Kate, looking at them, realized that she was seeing the new Flannery family. Nothing would ever be the same again.

The Water Lily was closed for the funeral, but Kate and her aunt kept it open the rest of the time, doing a slow but steady business. Supplies in the storeroom were disappearing, and there might not be more coming from Ireland. Kate had not yet told Ellen about the factory fire. How much bad news could one absorb in just a few days?

Aunt tired easily and could not be expected to help out every day for long, and Kate was not sure what she should do. She knew that Ellen was busy at the boardinghouse, trying to fill her mother's place there, when she was not at the hospital with Joe. She dared not ask what her plans for the shop were, not so soon.

Then she and Aunt Grace found a note stuck to the shop door one morning when they arrived to open it. "Come upstairs at once." The note was signed, "T. L. Woodmark."

"Do you know what his initials stand for?" Kate asked her aunt. In a time when not much amused her, she laughed, remembering that she had never heard his first name. Everybody always called him "Woodmark." Not "Mr. Woodmark."

"I never gave the 'T' a thought." Aunt turned the key in the lock. "It's strange that everyone just calls him by his last name."

"Probably his first name is horrible. Tobias? Thaddeus?" Kate shook her head. "He's full of mystery."

Kate had not told her aunt about the journal, or the connection she had made between Dr. Logan's friend and the journal's author. She was not sure why. "I wonder why he wants us upstairs?" she said.

"You go. I can't manage those steps right now. I'm stiff as stone this morning."

Kate ran up the steps—and what she saw in the upper hall explained the note. Six wicker shipping trunks sat outside Mr. Woodmark's door. Her order had come! It might be the last, but it would give her time to make plans for the future.

She rapped on Mr. Woodmark's door and after a short wait, he answered.

"You've found your shipment," he said. "Somebody from the docks brought it to the shop, and since you weren't open yet, the deliveryman gave it to me."

"You paid the charges?" Kate asked.

"We'll settle up later," he said. "I'll bring the trunks down to you this afternoon, unless you need them immediately. Now aren't you sorry that you didn't rent the little storeroom?"

Kate thought for a moment, and then said, "I *am* sorry. If it's still available—if none of the others have taken it—then I believe that Aunt and I will rent it. All of a sudden I have a wonderful feeling that everything will work out."

He smiled down at her. "I think you're right, Miss Keely. Now, before you run off, have you and your aunt decided to come to the picnic?"

"You know about Miss Flannery's mother?" Kate asked.

He nodded soberly. "I was sorry to hear. I hope she and her brother received the flowers."

Kate, remembering the bouquet sent by Mr. Woodmark, said, "Yes. She'll write to thank you when she has time. I don't imagine that she would be able to join you, but I'll remind her anyway. And Aunt and I would like to come."

His smile grew wider. "We're like a family, you know. The people in the shops and the magazine. You'll enjoy yourself."

Kate went away, feeling as if she were skimming on tiptoe. In the midst of all the sadness, something bright and good had happened. Then, halfway down the stairs, she remembered the journal. She should have asked him about it before—but there would be time for that another day. First, she would have to plan a way to admit that she had read most of it, and that would be hard to do.

If it was his, of course. But perhaps it wasn't! Perhaps she would never know who the writer was, that mysterious man who loved books and poetry—and his home.

Never knowing would be so much easier.

That night she took out the journal again and read the last entry.

West from Ogden, on the train: A compartment is so much better than what I have, but all of them had been secured by other passengers. I have caught a chill and do not remember ever feeling worse than I do now. To make the journey even more uncomfortable, I have discovered that the man sitting next to me has a revolver in a holster under his coat. I decided that I should come forward and ask him about his weapon, and he explained that two trains have been robbed in recent weeks after they left Ogden. "By passengers?" I asked, not believing this. What would a passenger do after robbing his fellow sufferers, return to his seat and read his newspaper? But no, he explained that the villains board the trains at meal stops, rob the passengers at gunpoint, and then jump off and disappear. My fellow traveler feels confident that he can defend himself, at least. Oh, when will this wretched trip be finished?

Soon we will stop for dinner, but I do not feel well enough to eat, especially since most of the food we find at the stations is not particularly good. I asked the conductor if any of the people with compartments will be leaving at the next stop, because I need more comfort that this seat provides, but he said that everyone was staying on to Oakland. I long for familiar—

The journal ended abruptly.

That was when the robbers boarded the train, Kate thought, shivering. Of course the journal's author was Mr. Woodmark.

I should destroy this, Kate thought, holding the journal with both hands. Then no one would know that I've read it.

I've spied on him. And he is the kind of man who would not want anyone to know his feelings.

And then there is *Isabel.*

Chapter 12

ELLEN

After the first terrible confusion, the boardinghouse took on a different life, one that Ellen could never have imagined. It was a strangely quiet place now, and for the first time Ellen realized that her mother's voice always had been heard all through the day, a comforting, low-key drone, as she went about the business of caring for a large house full of people who did not particularly want to settle their differences or compromise on any but the smallest disputes, or do without anything they had had the day before.

"Now, Luke," Ma would say to the elder McCarthy brother, "Matt's laundry didn't come back yesterday, so you let him wear one of your shirts. Yes, I mean it! You're lucky to have a brother." Or, "No, Mrs. Stackhouse, we will not have fish on Monday and Wednesday. Friday is enough. Everybody hates it but you." Or, "Is anybody going past the butcher shop? Mr. Delaney? Will you pick up two pounds of sliced ham and tell him to put it in my book?"

Or, "Ellen, girl, will you listen for once? The world isn't such a bad place, if you remember that heaven comes next."

Oh, Ma, if you're in heaven with Pa, then maybe I can believe you, Ellen thought one morning as she splashed cold water on her face after the alarm went off at five. The hourly routine of the house remained almost the same, but now it was Ellen who rose first, to wake Mary Clare in her small room next to the kitchen. Hugh came down as always to start the fires, but now it was Ellen who gave him his first cup of coffee, prepared on the small gas range. Now it was Ellen who shopped for food with Mary Clare after morning mass. And it was Ellen who counted linens before and after the weekly laundry deliveries. And Ellen who planned menus, collected money, and paid bills. And Ellen who went to the hospital to see Joe twice a day, without fail, and tried to reassure him that yes, there was all this pain, and yes, it was very frightening, but one day he would be home again and walking again, and everything would be the way it was before. Almost.

"I haven't been to The Water Lily for weeks," Ellen said to Mary Clare one Saturday morning as they shared kitchen chores. "I can't go on sending messages to Kate and asking for a little more time, especially now that she's so worried because the factory in Ireland burned down."

"She knows how hard you have it right now," Mary Clare said. "She can handle the shop, her and her aunt."

"I *can't* handle it *here*," Ellen said. "How did Ma manage? How do *you*? I've never worked so hard in my life."

"Sure, but don't we always take off our shoes and put our feet up every afternoon?" Mary Clare said as she wrung out a dishtowel, snapped the wrinkles out of it, and hung it on the string that stretched over the wood and coal range.

"For fifteen minutes," Ellen scoffed. She pressed one hand against the small of her back and sighed. "I'm going to run over to the shop this morning for a few minutes. Can you manage without me?"

"I'll get Thalia to help me set up the dining room for lunch," Mary Clare said. She brushed her hair out of her eyes with one water-wrinkled hand. "She's been a good girl. She does the vegetables as well as anybody else, and without much complaining, either."

"We can count on her for now, but what happens after school starts? That's not so long away." She sat down at the table and leaned on her elbows. "I suppose I should start thinking about hiring somebody."

Mary Clare scowled. "I can do anything your mother did. With a little help with meals and somebody to do the rooms—you or Thalia or Mrs. Stackhouse—then we wouldn't need to hire a stranger."

"Mrs. Stackhouse!" Ellen laughed.

"Who do you think made those applesauce cakes?" Mary Clare asked. "I didn't."

Ellen stared at her. "You're joking. Why didn't you tell me?"

"I forgot. But she's lonely, with your ma gone and all. She even misses Joe, and who would have thought it? So wouldn't we be better off with the devil we know than the devil we don't? I'll bet you a penny that if you asked her to help out—and cut her rent—she would."

Ellen shook her head. "She's impossible. And *she* doesn't pay her rent. Her son does." There were crumbs on the table, and she scraped them together in a little pile.

"And she feels guilty about it, too. I heard her telling him that the last time he was here. They were talking on the porch, and she says, 'Ed, I feel so bad that I'm costing you so much, so maybe I better go home with you and help Bernice keep house,' and he says, 'I won't hear another word.' So there."

Mary Clare was an inexhaustible source of information, Ellen knew. But this was a revelation, and a pathetic one. "Oh, dear. Now I almost feel sorry for her. Obviously her son and daughter-in-law don't want her with them."

"Well, who would?" practical Mary Clare said as she sat down at last with a cool cup of tea. "But she's *our* devil, so we might as well make the most of it. Ask her to do the rooms. She loves to snoop, but I don't think she steals. And maybe we can tire her out so she don't talk so much. She makes my head buzz sometimes."

And then Ellen laughed for the first time since she buried her mother.

She rushed into the shop a few minutes before eleven, and found Kate, her aunt, and Adele Carson there. Kate looked up from folding napkins to smile in welcome.

"Here you are! How are you feeling?"

"Fine, except for the sack of guilt I'm dragging around behind me. Have you been managing all right here?"

"Yes. As you can imagine, we haven't been stampeded with business, so Aunt and I have been handling it all very well."

"Hello, Adele," Ellen said, trying hard to add warmth to her voice, for she remembered Adele's kindness after the burial. "What brings you here? The need for dozens of new petticoats, I hope."

"Two," Adele said, holding up her choices. "And some news you might like. Kate told me that the factory that made your lovely things has gone out of business. It so happens that Edith's new brother-in-law has opened a dry goods emporium, and he has bolts and bolts of wonderful linen."

"Show her the scrap you brought in," Kate said. "Look at that, Ellen!"

Adele handed a handkerchief-sized piece of material to Ellen, and Ellen examined it closely. "Heavens, linen cambric. It's beautiful! It would be perfect for us."

"And this," Adele said, showing Ellen a piece of heavy dark blue linen. "He has it in green and maroon, too. And half a dozen other weights and colors. You should go by the store and see. He's anxious to build up his trade, and I'm sure he would work with you on prices."

Ellen liked what she saw, but there was a sadness about the whole thing. How could Kate smile at the idea of The Water Lily selling things made of linen that did not come from the factory in Ireland?

"I'm almost afraid to ask," she said, "but where is it made?"

Adele laughed aloud. "In Ireland. Now what do you think of that?"

Ellen shook her head, smiling. "That makes me feel better. What would two Irish girls be doing selling linen that came from somewhere else?"

"So will you come and look?" Adele asked. "I didn't promise him anything, of course, but I know he's eager to talk to you."

"Kate," Ellen said, imploring her friend. "You know I don't have time to even help you here, much less help you sew. The boardinghouse won't run itself, and I don't have a minute to spare. I really came to ask you if you would consider hiring someone to replace me, at least in the afternoons when you're busiest."

Kate was silent for a moment, looking over Ellen's

shoulder. Ellen was well aware that Miss Keely and Adele were waiting for her answer, too.

"You're talking as if I'm the only owner of the shop," Kate said slowly. "As if you were my employee."

Miss Keely excused herself suddenly and disappeared behind the curtain separating the shop from the storeroom. Adele developed a deep interest in hemstitched handkerchiefs displayed at the far end of the counter.

"You know that you really are the owner," Ellen said softly. The words were hard to say. "Most of the money came from you."

"And half of the work came from you—and more from your brothers, when we were getting the shop ready. I can't just replace you with hired help, Ellen," Kate said patiently. "Have you thought about hiring someone to help at the boardinghouse?"

"I have, but Mary Clare had a fit. And after I thought about it for a moment, I realized that I could never do that. Somehow . . . somehow it would be saying good-bye to Ma forever if I did that. I need to be there for the older boarders, and for Hugh, and even for Thalia. And for Joe, of course, when he gets home. You should hire someone, Kate, and pay her out of my share of the profit."

Kate looked down at her clasped hands, sighed, and finally said, "I'll need to do something. Aunt gets tired, being here every day."

Ellen leaned close to her. "What about Adele?"

Kate lifted an eyebrow. "I meant to talk to you about it. She might be willing. She's not wildly happy with the typing class her grandfather put her in."

"Then let's do it now," Ellen said. "Adele? Adele, would you like to take my place here in the afternoons? For the time being, anyway. You could still keep on with your typing class in the mornings, if that's what you really want."

Adele nodded and exclaimed, "Oh, I was hoping you'd ask. I thought that maybe you would if I told you about the dry goods emporium's linen!"

"Then consider it done," Kate said, and Ellen, suddenly tearful, pressed her cheek against Adele's and said, "Thank you. I won't forget that you helped us out."

To herself, she wondered if the girl she had embraced would one day be her sister-in-law—and suddenly she liked the idea. Oh, yes, Kate would have been perfect for Hugh. But he seemed to like Adele—and she was sweet and helpful. Typing? She apparently did not like it, and her grandfather would forget about it. A nice job in a small shop, then marriage, and then Ellen would have nieces and nephews to spoil at Sunday dinners in the boardinghouse.

She was halfway home before she realized the path her thoughts had traveled, and there on the windblown street of the city where she had been born, she knew where the path led.

That night she took out the silver locket Kate had given her and put it on. She would never remove it.

~

Thalia was accused of stealing shirt studs from Mr. Arbuckle's room, and the boardinghouse was in an uproar for a day and a half. Thalia, of course, denied it shrilly. Her room on the third floor was searched while she stood weeping in the doorway, and no shirt studs were found. The girl owned very little, so the search did not take long. Ellen's face burned the entire time, but the wrathful Mr. Arbuckle stood in the middle of the room grumbling. When Ellen found a small wooden box on the shelf in the corner, he shouted, "They're in that box!"

The box contained Joe's Sunday tie, carefully folded, and nothing else.

Ellen put the box back and blinked to keep tears out of her eyes. So Thalia was a thief, after all. But nothing would be said about the tie, at least until Joe was home.

"The shirt studs are not here," Ellen told Mr. Arbuckle, "and I'm not going to search every room in this house looking for them. Probably you left them in the shirt when it went to the laundry. Mr. Lee is very trustworthy. If he finds them, he will return them with the laundry. Now I don't want to hear anything more about it."

"You can't expect to keep boarders if you treat them like that!" the man blustered.

"Well, we don't expect to keep *you* at all!" Mrs. Stackhouse cried furiously. She had come late to the scene and still wore her long black coat. She had gone to the bakery for Ellen and had not been expected back for another half hour. "You, you can just pack up and leave if you can't keep a civil tongue!" Mrs. Stackhouse said, and she poked the man's arm with a fat finger. "Go along now. You've done enough harm."

The man left, and the room suddenly seemed to have more air in it. Thalia burst into noisy sobs and threw herself facedown on her narrow bed. Mrs. Stackhouse patted her bony shoulder, flapped the thin quilt over her, and told her to rest for an hour and then, "Come down to the kitchen and polish the spoons, like I told you twice over."

Inwardly, Ellen sighed. Mrs. Stackhouse, asked to help out, had assumed charge of much of the boardinghouse, enraging Mary Clare and most of the boarders. Ellen would have to talk to her again.

She started down the stairs behind the woman, hearing, with amazement, her mother's voice coming out of her own mouth. "I surely do appreciate your help, Mrs. Stackhouse, but I believe that the boarders—and Thalia, too—will take directions from me better than anyone else. You don't want them to think you're the one taking Ma's place, do you? No, I knew you wouldn't presume any such thing, you being so sensitive and all. Now tell me, did the baker have the rolls I ordered?"

Mrs. Stackhouse, diverted, launched a lengthy complaint about the careless baker, and the difficult moment passed. Ellen responded with assurances of speaking to the baker the next day without fail, and for a moment, at the foot of the stairs, she thought she heard her mother's footsteps behind her.

But no one was there.

Kate came in a few days later to tell her about the picnic at Mr. Woodmark's country place, and about the poets and writers she met, and the children of the shopkeepers, and the sweet Portuguese family that maintained the place and cared for the cows.

"And the land goes right down to the sea, Ellen," Kate said, her eyes bright. "You should have seen the waves crashing in. For a moment I almost thought I was in Ireland again, but then I turned around, and there were the yellow hills behind me, and that Spanish-y house with the courtyard fountain that belongs to Mr. Woodmark."

She's almost in love, Ellen thought wistfully.

Everything has passed me by. But yet—but yet, she wondered, am I not more contented now than I have ever been? How could that be?

"I'm glad you had a good time," she told Kate. "You're sunburned, too. Put a little butter on it so you don't peel."

"Do you know how much you sound like your mother?" Kate asked, as if surprised.

"So I hear," Ellen said, laughing a little. "The boarders

thought they'd have an easier time with me, about leaving their things scattered around and not paying on time. They've been surprised."

"And the McCarthy boys? Do they mind you?"

"Of course not. You know that Luke is going to marry Mary McFee, don't you?"

"That can't be true! I saw Hugh two days ago, and he didn't say a word." Kate was scowling now, and Ellen thought she knew why. Kate had picked Luke for her. The two of them might have sworn not to marry for years, but each had made plans for the other.

"Hugh's trying to pretend that it won't happen. He doesn't want more changes. And neither do I, for that matter. But the McCarthys were moving out in September anyway. They found wonderful new jobs up the coast, and Mary's going with them. So we'll have new people moving in, and the first thing I'm going to do is raise the rents all around. This bunch can afford it, and the price of food is going up every week."

"That's your mother talking again," Kate said, and her eyes filled with tears.

"Don't you dare cry. Now tell me about the shop. How is Adele working out?"

"Oh, she's a perfect salesgirl. And she knows everything about sewing, so she's going to make two petticoats a week for us. And Edith wants to sew for us, too. She said she never wanted to make another shirtwaist as long as she lived, but she doesn't mind drawers and nightgowns, as long as she can work at home."

Ellen narrowed her eyes. "You've become a whole industry, Kate. And you're barely eighteen. What next?"

"Next, I'm going to find a couple of other women who like to sew who'll do pieces for us—and I hope I don't have union problems. Hugh says I'd better be careful or I will. But you know how he is."

"I do—and I'll handle him. Don't you worry."

"Ellen, I hear your mother again," Kate said. "I'd better be going or I'll be weeping on your shoulder. How can you be so brave?"

"Morning mass and Mary Clare banging pots in the kitchen," Ellen said. "Ma always did say those two things kept her from having spells or vapors or any of the other ailments that are in fashion."

Kate left, and Ellen hurried to the kitchen. Mary Clare was teaching Thalia to slice bread evenly—and losing patience. "No, watch me again. Line up the raw end of the loaf with this scratch on the bread board, and then line up the knife with that scratch on the board. . . ."

Ellen stirred the pot of beans and then poured herself a cup of coffee. Leaning against the kitchen table, she sipped it and said, "Thalia, what are we going to do about school clothes for you? I say we just start you in with the sisters, and you can wear nice little dark blue uniforms like the other girls, and then we won't have to worry about a thing. And you'll learn such lovely manners there."

Thalia, scowling over bread, said, "Uniforms cost a lot."

"You've earned it," Ellen said. "And we'll get two pairs of shoes and a good dark blue coat, too, maybe with a red lining and brass buttons."

Thalia raised a smiling face. "And a church dress?"

"Don't push me," Ellen said. "Finish with the bread, and I'll show you how to make crowns out of the napkins."

In the distant front hall, Mrs. Stackhouse was scolding someone for not wiping his feet before he came in. Hugh banged in the back door, carrying a coal scuttle in each hand. Someone answered the ringing telephone, and upstairs, someone else began singing loudly.

"Them potatoes have got sprouts again," Mary Clare said disgustedly, peering into the box in the pantry. "And there isn't but half a dozen carrots left."

"Mr. Lee is here with the laundry!" Thalia yelled, as someone rapped on the back door.

"You're wanted on the phone, Ellen," Mrs. Stackhouse said. "I didn't get the name."

Ellen, examining potatoes in the pantry, said, "I can't come now. Can you take a message?"

"Maybe he wants a room," Mrs. Stackhouse said, without any particular interest. "I'll just tell him to ring back some other time. But it sounded like that nice-looking

German fellow with the poor little motherless boy that Father McLean introduced you to after mass the other day." She started back to the phone. "Then I'll set the tables."

"Count the laundry first—and look for those wretched shirt studs, please," Ellen said. "I don't want to hear another word about shirt studs if I live to be a hundred."

Why was that man—what was his name?—calling at this time of day? she wondered vaguely. Was he the one that the priest said needed a room? The potatoes were usable—but Mary Clare could cook macaroni, too. No one would mind when they were having such good roast beef for dinner.

With luck, she would be in bed by midnight.

Chapter 13

KATE

"So I got the surprise of my life when I dropped by the boardinghouse the other day," Kate was saying as she waded in the shallow water. "Ellen had set up three sewing machines in the empty room, and there was Edith with two of Adele's school friends, too busy to do much more than look up when I walked in." The incoming tide lapped at her skirt and she lifted it up another discreet inch.

Beside her, his trousers rolled up halfway to his knees, splashing along in apparent satisfaction, Mr. Woodmark nodded and said, "She's turning the place into a sort of factory, then."

"Well, not quite," Kate said. "But she's got Thalia involved, too, after school. She keeps the floor swept clean and gathers up the pins and scraps."

"That's the girl who didn't like you," Mr. Woodhouse said. "Quite unreasonable." He bent to pick up a shell and handed it to Kate.

"Oh, Thalia still doesn't like me," Kate said, examining the shell. "And—shame on me—I don't much like her, either. But she adores Ellen, and Ellen treats her like a daughter, so harmony prevails."

He looked straight at her then, smiling, the sun reflecting off his glasses. "'Harmony prevails.' You love that, don't you?"

"Who doesn't?" Kate said. "Isn't it what we all want? We'd better walk back toward the house. Aunt has probably taken over your kitchen by now."

"I don't think so. When we left, I saw that she was being enchanted by Mr. Roland, out on the patio."

Kate laughed happily. "Of course, because he's a real poet and he looks the part, too. All that white hair and the walking stick. Aunt hasn't had such a good time since my father was alive and always bringing writers and poets to the house for Sunday dinner."

Mr. Woodmark, watching his steps, said, "I never met your father, but my father asked him to write something for *High Tide*. I don't think he ever did. But your friend Peter Prescott sent me an inquiry not long ago. I've never met him, either, but he's heard that we're starting the magazine up again, and I remember that he wrote interesting articles for *The Call* from time to time. How many chances you and I had to meet, and yet we never did."

You have no idea, Kate thought, not certain whether to be dismayed or not. If he meets Peter—and learns that we all returned to San Francisco on the same train—and Peter says something about the journal . . . She could not finish the thought.

Suddenly what had seemed to be a little romantic and quite intriguing appeared to be perilous. She had brought the journal with her and meant to give it to him sometime during the day—and admit that she had read it—but so far, halfway through Sunday, she had not found the right opportunity. Now the hoped-for opportunity was turning into something else, something potentially embarrassing.

How can I admit that I have read his thoughts? she wondered. There did not seem to be an easy way. But what if he meets Peter and the two of them start talking? "You were away from the city? So was I! When did you return? Why, I was on the same train!" Kate could imagine the entire conversation.

They turned back, found their shoes, and climbed the hill to the sprawling old farmhouse, where discolored plaster walls were dappled with shadows from the overhanging trees. The September day had been too warm for comfort, and now the sun was low in the sky, blazing and harsh. Two of the farm dogs ran down to meet them, ingratiating themselves by curling around their legs and whimpering. "Your aunt doesn't really like country life, does she?" Mr. Woodmark asked suddenly. "She only came to chaperone you."

"She liked coming out here for your picnic," Kate protested. "And I couldn't have kept her away today! But she does love the city."

"I love both." Mr. Woodhouse did not look at her. "And you?"

Kate sighed. "I don't know. The city is too full of bad memories—they take me by surprise sometimes. Remember the other day when it was so windy? I was halfway home when I remembered the strange winds during the big fire. There was a kind of rushing and roaring and howling that would come up when both sides of a street burned at the same time. We were in too much danger to be frightened, if that makes any sense. We just didn't have time to be afraid, and now, years afterward, sometimes I *am* afraid." She laughed a little. "Why am I telling you this? We never talk about it, Ellen or Hugh or Aunt and I. And I never hear other people talking about it, either. Sometimes I think it's as if we're all ashamed of having had such a terrible thing happen to us, as if we were somehow negligent and deserved it."

"I'm glad you can talk to me," he said. "I was in Berkeley then, and I don't like remembering those times, either, even though I was quite safe."

They had reached the shaded patio, where Aunt and another woman were setting the long table for dinner. The elderly poet sat nearby, watching them and occasionally directing an approving remark to Aunt. Kate took her shoes indoors, to the privacy of the small upstairs bedroom he had turned over to her and her aunt as a place to leave their coats and hats, and where Kate had left her stockings earlier. She brushed the sand off her feet and legs, put on her stockings, and attempted to tidy her windblown hair in a small mirror.

Ten people were at the place, counting the two servants. Somehow she should find a private moment to return the journal to her host, but the speech she had planned seemed foolish. "This was given to me by mistake, and I only read it to see if I could identify the owner. . . ." Ridiculous. He would consider her a snoop. It would have been better if she had thrown it away—before she had read it.

But then, if Peter tells him about it? She did not want to lose the respect of Mr. Woodmark, and she did not dare wonder why.

Going home on the ferry, the party stood together at the rail and admired the city as they approached it. "It's the best place in the world," Aunt said softly, at Kate's elbow.

"Yes, Aunt," Kate said, not sure at all. She slid her hand into her coat pocket and felt the journal there, wanting to give it to Mr. Woodmark before saying good-bye to him that night and knowing that she would not. She did not have the words to explain.

A comfortable routine at the shop was established. Kate, Adele, and Aunt kept it open and sold both the last of the goods sent from Ireland and the new things made in the boardinghouse. The slow but steady supply met the shop's needs, and they were successful enough to begin making plans for holiday windows and a small newspaper advertisement. Mr. Woodmark even planned to put a short article about them in his magazine.

"Not that we need it," Adele said. "Having the college women discover us was such a blessing. One of them told me that we cover more collegiate behinds than anyone else."

Kate laughed, but Aunt gasped. "Girls, girls, let's not make jokes like that, especially when someone is in the dressing room."

Kate and Adele apologized, but moments later, when their solitary customer came out of the dressing room carrying the skirt she planned to buy, she said, "It's not only collegiate behinds you're covering. You're becoming the secret 'smart' place to buy. It won't be much longer before The Water Lily is all the fashion."

Adele had the grace to blush, but Kate's mind was busy with this information. It was good news—the best news. Aunt had assured her often that they would be fortunate if they became a fashionable place, one where the important women in the city shopped. Even though their fame might not last long among such fickle people, the shop name would remain familiar, and whenever someone wanted something very special, The Water Lily would be where they went.

"If our supply lasts," she finished.

"Ellen swears that it will," Kate said. "She says she could easily find another two or three women to sew, if she had the room and if we could sell the things. Plenty of women would like working a few mornings or afternoons a week, especially if the surroundings are pleasant."

When the customer left, Adele said, "Imagine being a seamstress and choosing your own hours and being able to go to the lavatory anytime you like."

"Couldn't you? I mean go to the lavatory, back in the shirtwaist factory?" Aunt asked, frowning.

"Certainly not! We couldn't leave our machines for any reason. We brought our lunches from home and ate them at our places, with the supervisor running back and forth behind us yelling at us to get back to work. Anyone who needed a lavatory break was fired. There was always somebody else with better kidneys who wanted the job."

"Hugh says unions will change all of that," Kate said.

"And he's right, too. But he's careful about his union talk around Ellen. She told him that if he kept bringing it up, she'd give him such a smack that he'd remember it to his dying day." Adele laughed while telling them this.

"She's getting more like her mother every day," Aunt said. "It's a transformation I wouldn't believe if I were not watching it happen."

"That family has been through so much," Adele said. "Sometimes, when Hugh talks about the earthquake—"

Kate did not hear anything else. Hugh *talks* to her about that terrible time? She barely could believe it.

"It was difficult for everyone," Aunt said in a tone that meant that she did not want to hear any more on the subject. "Girls, I'm a little tired. We're not very busy, so would you mind if I ran along home?" She already was untying her apron.

"Go ahead. It's past three," Kate said. "Adele and I can manage the thundering herds, if there are any. But do you feel well enough to stop for bread?"

"Certainly. And I'm going to stop by the bookstore, too. They are holding something for me."

After Aunt left, Kate said, "I'll bet Aunt is picking up a book of poetry."

Adele, unpacking a flat box of napkins and setting them on a shelf, said, "Something by that old gentleman who takes her out to lunch?"

"The very one. I detect a grand passion."

Adele had a wonderful laugh, and Kate, hearing it again, suspected that more than one grand passion was going on under her nose. Hugh must love that laugh, she thought. How it must light up the boardinghouse when she is there.

She spent a few moments in the storeroom with a needle, catching a few loose threads on a petticoat and thinking that the rough edges of many lives were mending now, sometimes in unexpected ways. It was about time.

That evening, she read through several newspapers that Aunt had saved for her until she had time for them. Kate rarely bothered with the gossip columns, but a photo and a name caught her attention as she was turning a page. Aaron Schuster! According to the article, he was leaving—had already left, according to the date!—for a place called Wheatplain, Kansas, where he would be the assistant to his uncle in another Schuster store. The article was short, almost begrudging, and the photo was small. Aaron looked rather heavy, his collar was too tight, and his smile was forced. Kate could not resist a smirk. Assistant. What did that mean? Clerk? Whatever had happened in his life must not have been good, for him to be shunted aside to a relative's store in a tiny town so far away. He would be forgotten soon enough in faithless San Francisco. Had Ellen seen this? Probably not. But Kate decided that she would not ask.

What Kate had dreaded finally came to pass. One afternoon, while she was rearranging the window display, she saw Peter Prescott going past, on his way to the doorway leading upstairs to Mr. Woodmark's flat.

He and Mr. Woodmark will talk about their travels, she thought, and one thing will lead to another, and Peter will tell him when we arrived back in San Francisco. So far all Mr. Woodmark knew was that Kate had returned from Ireland before the winter holidays. She tried to watch the sidewalk, to see Peter leave, but the shop suddenly became busy around four o'clock, and she did not have an opportunity to look out again until closing time. She imagined all sorts of conversations going on upstairs, and all of them ended with Peter's revelation that he had given a lost journal to Kate to read on the train.

Kate needed to talk to someone about this. Ellen perhaps? Would she have time to listen, or any sympathy for the problem?

After dinner, she left Aunt reading poetry by the living room window and hurried to the boardinghouse, in time to catch Ellen in the kitchen, supervising the washing-up while she stirred gingerbread batter in a big yellow bowl.

"Here you are!" Ellen exclaimed, as if she had been expecting Kate for hours. "Thalia, pour Kate a cup of tea. Mary Clare, is there a piece of that apple pie left? Good. Give it to Kate."

Kate sat down, unbuttoning her coat, and Thalia set a cup of tea in front of her silently. "How are you, Thalia?" Kate murmured politely.

"Fine," Thalia barked, and she left the room abruptly.

Kate sighed. "Honestly. When is she going to get over hating me?"

"Never," Mary Clare said as she gave Kate the pie and a napkin. "She carries a grudge like an old maid."

"Thank you," Ellen said wryly. "Speak for yourself, *miss*. But with the sort of life we're leading, what else could we be, Mary Clare?" She poured the gingerbread batter into a large sheet pan and slid it into the oven, then wiped her hands on her apron and sat down with Kate. "What brings you here tonight, Kate?"

"I need somebody to talk to," Kate said.

Mary Clare abandoned the rest of the dishes, sat down at the table, too, and leaned on her elbows. Kate, ready to ask her to leave, decided against it. Mary Clare had been a part of her life for a long time, and she had common sense.

"Here's what's happened," Kate began. The other two leaned closer—and Kate felt as if she were being suddenly embraced.

This is a good house, she thought. A safe one. I'm lucky to be able to call these women my friends.

When she left an hour later, she nearly bumped into a neatly dressed man on the porch steps. He said, "Pardon me, please," in heavily accented English, and he rang the bell as Kate turned up the sidewalk. A potential new boarder? Kate wondered, looking back at him. Did Ellen still have room? Goodness, I hope so! she thought. Nice looking, with good clothes, and polite, too. As she hurried away, she smiled.

Aunt was already in her nightgown when Kate reached home. She was sitting on the edge of her bed, braiding her hair, when Kate looked in on her, and the first thing she said, after greeting her niece, was, "Do you think we need a telephone?"

Kate, surprised, said, "Why? Practically the only person we know with a telephone is Ellen, and she almost has to keep one, in order to satisfy the boarders. And Mr. Woodmark has one—I hear it ringing upstairs sometimes."

"Think how convenient a telephone could be," Aunt said as she snapped an elastic in place. "Instead of coming over to see us and taking a chance on our not being here, someone could telephone first."

"Hmm," Kate said. She took off her hat and shrugged out of her coat. "Who are you expecting?"

"I? No one, of course. Who comes to see me?" Aunt said innocently.

"Only half the women at church and your entire Ladies' Reading Association," Kate said. "All right, tell me who came and surprised you with your dressing gown on."

"Mr. Woodmark," Aunt said, with considerable satisfaction.

Kate's mouth went dry. Peter has told him, she thought.

"What did he want?" she asked.

"A visit with you, I suppose," Aunt said. "He didn't accept my invitation for coffee, so I assume I wasn't the one he came to see. And I was *not* in my dressing gown."

Kate sat down on the edge of the bed. "How did he seem?"

"Eager to see you," Aunt said. "Disappointed that you weren't here. He left a message, if you care to hear it."

"You're really enjoying this, aren't you?" Kate said, ready to laugh or cry, depending on the message.

"I admit that I am," Aunt said. "He said he would like to take you to lunch tomorrow, if you have time and if you are willing. I asked if this was a business matter, and he seemed horrified. No, no, he said. Not business. So I asked if it was a social occasion, and he calmed himself down enough to admit that it was. So I told him I would convey the message and he could ask you himself tomorrow at the shop. Are you satisfied?"

Kate got up. "I have no idea what you mean," she said, and she grabbed her hat and coat and went to her own room. Behind her, her aunt laughed.

What does he want? she wondered. Her room was not big enough to pace in, or she would have paced. Did Peter tell him?

Why didn't I tell him? I sound like a snoop, a silly woman who reads someone else's journal and keeps it a secret. But how was I to know it was his?

The truth is that there was no mistake, not after I heard about the attack on the train from Dr. Logan. And Mr. Woodmark once told me that he returned to San Francisco just before Christmas, and I sat there without a word.

I'll just tell him that I forgot I even had the journal!

No, I'll do what Ellen and Mary Clare told me to do. I'll confess to him before he has a chance to confront me, and I'll do it immediately. If we had a telephone, I'd do it tonight!

She lay awake a long time that night, with the journal on the bedside table beside her. Secrets spinning madly inside of secrets, she thought. I should have had enough of that when I was in Ireland. I kept Dr. Logan's secret, because it was merciful. Jolie didn't need to know how sick she was. I kept Jolie's secret that she was in love with David Fairfield, because her father did not need to know that she wanted to marry. And I kept my secret, because I was ashamed of wanting to abandon her once I reached Ireland. And ashamed of going with her in the first place only because I wanted the money her father had promised me.

I swore I would never do anything like that again.

I'll tell Mr. Woodmark tomorrow morning, before he asks me to go to lunch with him. And if he changes his mind, I deserve it.

She turned to her side and went to sleep.

~

Mr. Woodmark was prompt, appearing in the shop five minutes after it opened, before any customers arrived. Kate, seeing him, told Adele and Aunt that she was going outside for a moment with the man, and before he had a chance to protest, she rushed him outside.

"Here now," he said mildly. "I wasn't about to say something to ruin your reputation or cause your business to fail."

Kate thrust the journal at him. "This is yours. I've had it since I was on the train, the same train with you. You must have dropped it when you were taken off, after you were injured. Peter found it and thought it was mine, so I took it, and I admit that I read it."

She paused for breath. He took the journal and stared at her.

"I have no idea what you are talking about," he said. He looked down at the small leather book and shook his head. "I had forgotten all about it. Isn't this amazing? I've never kept a journal in my life, until this one, and I hadn't given it a thought until this moment."

She stood rigid, waiting for everything she had said to sink in on him. It did.

"You read it, you say?" he asked. His eyebrows rose. The one with the scar reminded her of what had happened to him.

"I did," she said. "I looked through it to see if there was a name." Liar, she thought. "Well, I started out that way, and then I became interested, because I really wanted to go home, too, but not for the same reasons you had. It wasn't that I missed San Francisco so much as that I had responsibilities here—and I had nowhere else to go."

"Ah," he said.

"And you write very well, so I liked that."

"I see," he said.

"And then I began wondering about you," she said. "And I wondered . . . I wondered . . ."

"Yes?"

"About Isabel," she said.

He looked away. "I don't remember what I wrote about her."

"It sounded as if she meant something to you."

"She meant something to my brother, but not enough," he said. He looked down at her and smiled suddenly. "I'd like to hope that you worried that she might mean something to me."

"I didn't even know who you were!" she said.

"Until . . . when?"

She closed her eyes to shut out the sight of him. "I don't really know when, exactly. Things fell into place. The robbery on the train—Dr. Logan told me about your part in fighting the robbers off—and just the way you write. You write like you talk."

When she glanced at him again, he was looking down the street, as if watching something. But the street, so early in the day, was nearly empty. "Would you have lunch with me? At twelve-thirty? Any place you like? We can sort everything out then." As he spoke, he slid the journal into the inside pocket of his coat. "And I'll tell you everything you want to know about Isabel."

"Yes," Kate said. "To everything."

"I hope you're always so agreeable, Miss Keely," he said.

"You may call me Kate," she said.

"Thank you, Kate." He hesitated a moment, as if he was going to say something. But then he smiled and walked away.

Kate, watching him, shook her head in amusement. "Woodmark," she whispered. She went back into the shop, smiling.

JEAN THESMAN is the author of many novels for teenagers. She is a member of the Authors Guild and the Society of Children's Book Writers and Illustrators, and lives in Washington State.

Visit her Web site at **www.jeanthesman.com**